DRIFT XTREME
HIGH PLAINS
DRIFTING

PRINCESS ADVENTURE STORIES

Disney PRESS
New York

TABLE OF CONTENTS

All illustrations by the Disney Storybook Artists.

For information address Disney Press, 114 Fifth Avenue, New York, New York 10011-5690.

First Edition

Printed in the United States of America

10 9 8 7 6 5 4 3 2 1

G942-9090-6-13238

Library of Congress Control Number: 2012954890

ISBN 978-1-4231-4691-9

Visit www.disneybooks.com

For Text Only

Beyond the Tower

Once upon a time, there was a magic golden flower that could heal the sick. A selfish woman named Mother Gothel found the flower and used its powers to keep herself young.

Nearby, there lived a good queen and a kind king. One day, the Queen grew ill. The only thing that could save her was the magic flower. So the King searched far and wide until he found it. The Queen was cured, and soon after, she gave birth to a baby girl named Rapunzel.

The infant's golden hair held the magic of the flower, and Mother Gothel wanted it. So one night, she crept into the castle and stole the princess.

The King and Queen were heartbroken, yet they never lost faith that their daughter would return. Every year on the night of her birthday, they released lanterns into the sky, hoping that the lights would lead Rapunzel home.

For nearly eighteen years, Mother Gothel raised Rapunzel in a tall, tall tower. Rapunzel's hair grew longer and longer, and when she sang, the blond locks would glow, keeping Mother Gothel looking young.

Scared to lose her magic, Mother Gothel convinced Rapunzel that people would harm her if she ever left the tower. And so Rapunzel stayed. She kept busy knitting and painting pictures, most of which included a beautiful sun. But there was one thing she wanted to do more than anything.

"I want to see the floating lights!" Rapunzel told Mother Gothel. "They appear every year on my birthday. I have to know what they are!"

Mother Gothel would have none of it. She told Rapunzel frightening tales of the world outside: men with pointy teeth, quicksand, and snakes.

Still, Rapunzel was determined to see the floating lights.

Rapunzel's chance came that very day when a stranger named Flynn Rider climbed her tower. The young man was a thief who had stolen a beautiful gold crown.

Scared that the stranger was there to steal the magic of her hair, Rapunzel used it to tie Flynn to a chair. Then she took Flynn's satchel with the crown and hid it.

When Rapunzel talked to Flynn, he didn't seem to know about her hair. But he did know about the lights. He told her they were lanterns. She decided to make a deal. "You will act as my guide, take me to these lanterns, and return me home safely. Then, and only then, will I return your satchel."

Flynn had no choice. He agreed.

Rapunzel was thrilled . . . until she remembered all the terrible things Mother Gothel had told her about life outside the tower. Then she looked at her painting of the floating lights. She wanted to see them so badly! Taking a deep breath, she climbed down out of her tower using her long golden hair.

When her feet touched the soft, green grass, she let out a happy cry. “I can’t believe I did this!”

As Rapunzel explored the forest for the first time, she was filled with joy. But she also felt guilty for disobeying Mother Gothel. One minute she was smiling and laughing. The next minute she was frowning.

Flynn was hoping Rapunzel wouldn't want to continue. But she was determined. "I'm going to see those lanterns!" she told him.

Flynn led Rapunzel to the Snuggly Duckling, a tavern full of thieves and thugs. Flynn was sure that as soon as Rapunzel took one step inside, she would be so scared, she'd run back to her tower. Then he could get the crown back and be on his way.

But Flynn's plan went wrong. The thugs recognized him from a "Wanted" poster. They decided to take him in for the reward.

"Put him down!" Rapunzel commanded. Surprised, the thugs let Flynn go. Then, Rapunzel explained how she needed Flynn to take her to the lights. "Haven't any of you ever had a dream?" she asked.

As it turned out, every one of the thugs had a dream. One wanted to be a concert pianist; another wanted to find true love. The list went on and on and on! Before long, the meanest, toughest men in the kingdom were singing with Rapunzel and swearing to do whatever they could to help her make her dream come true.

Suddenly, the palace guards appeared in the tavern, looking for Flynn. The thugs helped Rapunzel and Flynn escape. The pair ran until they came to a steep cliff. Rapunzel used her hair to swing them over. Then she used her hair's magic light to lead them through a dark, flooded cave.

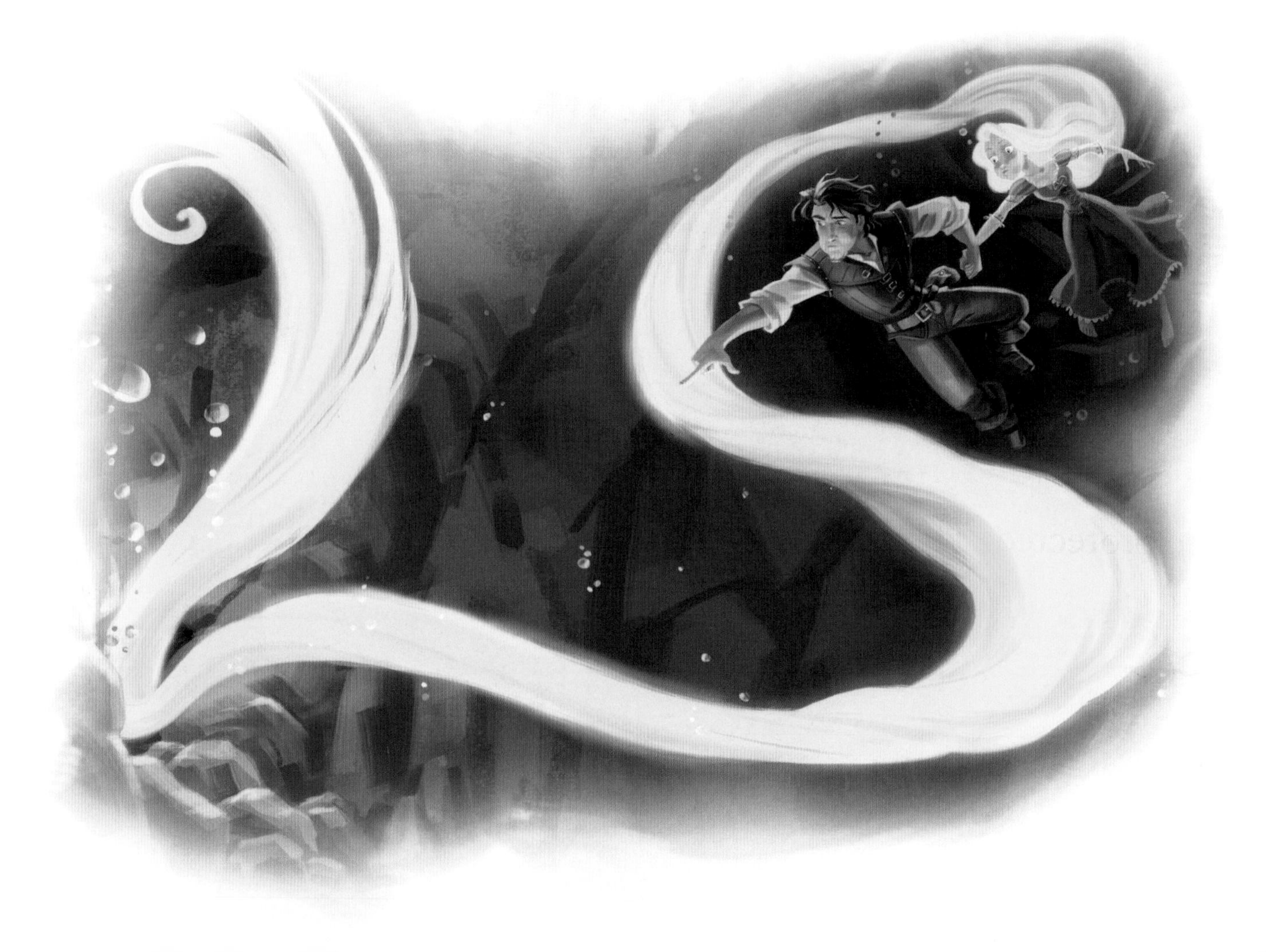

"Your hair glows . . . " Flynn said when they got safely to the shore. "I didn't see that coming."

"It doesn't just glow," Rapunzel calmly explained, wrapping her hair around a wound on his hand. Within moments, Flynn's palm was healed. "But once it's cut, it turns brown and loses its power. It has to be protected. That's why Mother never let me . . . "

"You never left the tower," Flynn finished for her. Now, Flynn understood why Rapunzel wanted to see the floating lights.

Later that night, when Flynn went to get firewood, Mother Gothel appeared. She tried to get Rapunzel to go back to the tower with her, but Rapunzel refused. "I've seen and learned so much," she explained. "I even met someone."

Mother Gothel laughed. She told Rapunzel that Flynn only wanted the crown back—he didn't care about her at all.

"Give it to him. You'll see," Mother Gothel promised.

Rapunzel knew Flynn was a good man. She would prove Mother Gothel wrong.

The next day, Rapunzel and Flynn reached the kingdom. As evening fell, Flynn rowed them out into the harbor to see the lanterns. Certain that Flynn was her friend, Rapunzel gave the crown back to him. "I should have given it to you before, but I was just scared," she said. "And the thing is, I'm not scared anymore."

Suddenly Flynn said he had to go ashore. "I'll be right back," he promised. But the next time Rapunzel saw Flynn, he was sailing away into the night. Her heart broke. Mother Gothel had been right.

Upset, Rapunzel returned to the tower. She couldn't stop thinking about everything she'd seen—especially a flag with a golden sun symbol. It was the same sun she'd used in her own paintings. Suddenly, it all became clear. . . .

"*I'm* the lost princess!" she told Mother Gothel, outraged. "You were wrong about the world, and you were wrong about me. I will never let you use my hair again."

Just then, Flynn appeared. He hadn't left Rapunzel on purpose. He'd been kidnapped! As soon as he'd gotten free, he raced to the tower.

Rapunzel was overjoyed—until Mother Gothel wounded Flynn with a knife.

Rapunzel rushed to his side to try to heal him. But just as she started to sing, Flynn took a shard of broken glass and cut off her magic hair. Instantly, it turned brown . . . and Mother Gothel turned to dust.

A tear fell from Rapunzel's eye as she realized she couldn't save Flynn. As soon as the tear touched Flynn's cheek, his wound began to heal. Rapunzel's hair was no longer magic—but there was still power inside of her!

There was one thing left to do. Together, Rapunzel and Flynn rode straight to the castle, where they found the King and Queen. Rapunzel's parents knew her at once. They were thrilled. Their long-lost princess had finally returned.

Rapunzel's life had changed so quickly. She had gotten herself out of the tower, saved Flynn, and found her true family.

Now, she was right where she was meant to be.

Runaway Rajah

Everywhere Aladdin and Jasmine turned, something spectacular caught their eye. It was the biggest parade of the year, and it seemed as though everyone in Agrabah had turned out to see it.

"Look, Aladdin, a snake charmer!" Jasmine cried.

"And over there." Aladdin pointed. "A fire-eater!"

As always, Rajah was by Jasmine's side. The tiger let out a soft roar. "*Rrrr!*"

A group of peacocks strutted by. Next came elephants draped in silk and strings of pearls. Then several camels walked by, bells jangling from their halters. But Jasmine couldn't take her eyes off the group of tigers. They were magnificent!

A young girl was leading the tigers. After a few moments, the girl tossed a melon to one of the beautiful beasts. The tiger caught it with his teeth, flipped it up, and balanced it on his nose.

Aladdin whistled softly. "Impressive," he said.

Jasmine smiled. "That's good, but you should see what Rajah can do." She stroked the tiger's fur. "Shall we show them?"

Rajah gave a happy rumble.

Jasmine bought some fruit from a nearby stall and put it in a bowl. She tossed a melon to Rajah. He flipped it up to his

nose. Then Jasmine tossed him an apple and a fig. Rajah balanced both on top of the melon!

Aladdin started to applaud, but Jasmine held up her hand.

At Jasmine's signal, Rajah flung the fruit into the air. *Whoosh!* He sliced it into pieces with his claws.

Jasmine caught the pieces in the bowl as they fell.

"Rajah, you're good enough to be in the parade," Aladdin exclaimed.

"Speaking of joining parades . . ." Jasmine smiled. She pointed at Abu, who was eagerly watching a group of female monkeys go past with their trainers. "It looks as if Abu wants to stay for a while longer."

Aladdin laughed. "Okay," he said. "Abu, why don't you and Rajah walk along with the parade? Jasmine and I will take a stroll through the marketplace and meet you back at the palace."

A little while later, Jasmine and Aladdin returned to the palace. They looked for their friends, but Rajah and Abu were nowhere to be found.

"That's odd," said Jasmine. "I thought they'd be back by now."

Aladdin ran a hand through his hair. "Maybe they wanted to follow the parade to the end. After all, it will be moving on to another city tonight."

Just then, Abu ran into the palace gardens. He tugged on Jasmine's outfit. He looked upset!

"Abu," Jasmine said, worried, "what's wrong?"

Abu leaped up onto the rim of the nearby garden fountain. He acted out strutting like a peacock, walking like an elephant, and dancing like a pretty girl.

"Something happened at the parade?" Aladdin guessed.

Abu nodded eagerly. Then he swished his tail like a tiger.

"Something happened to Rajah!" Jasmine exclaimed.

Abu found a bracelet and slipped it over his neck like a collar.

Jasmine's eyes widened. "Rajah's been taken by the parade folks! If we don't find him soon, they'll take him to the next city." She turned to Aladdin. "Quick, where's the Magic Carpet?"

Within minutes, Jasmine, Aladdin, and Abu were soaring over the city.

"Hurry, Carpet!" Aladdin urged. "We need to catch up to the parade before everyone in it leaves."

They flew this way and that. Finally, they spotted an elephant. "Over there!" Aladdin exclaimed. "To the left, I see it."

The Magic Carpet saluted with its tassels and turned sharply, throwing its passengers off balance. Aladdin and Jasmine held on, but Abu tumbled off the edge.

Just as he fell, Jasmine snatched him back.

"Gotcha!" she cried. She pulled the little monkey to safety. "I don't want to lose any more of our friends today."

The Carpet continued toward the part of the city where Aladdin had spotted the parade.

"Watch out!" Aladdin cried as they dropped between the buildings. The Magic Carpet tried to stop, but it crashed into a bunch of clotheslines. Aladdin, Jasmine, and Abu tumbled safely off onto a nearby rooftop. But the Carpet was all tangled up!

"We need to keep moving," Jasmine said. "Abu, you stay here and help Carpet. Aladdin, come with me. We have to get to the parade!"

Jasmine went to the corner of the roof and listened carefully. With the other buildings blocking her view, she couldn't see the parade anymore. But she could still hear it.

"I think it's over there," she said, pointing. "We'll make our own shortcut." She grabbed a long pole and quickly vaulted from one rooftop to the next. Each time, she threw the pole back to Aladdin so he could follow.

Finally, they reached the building just before the end of the parade. Three stories below, they could see the animals being loaded into carts, getting ready to move to the next city. Jasmine saw the peacocks, the elephants—and yes—the tigers!

"Oh, no!" Jasmine gasped when she spotted Rajah. "They're putting the tigers into cages. We have to stop them."

Aladdin nodded. "But we're so high up. What's the quickest way to get down?"

"The quickest way," Jasmine repeated with a gleam in her eyes. "Do you trust me?"

"Of course," Aladdin said.

"Then—JUMP!" Jasmine clasped his hand, and they leaped from the rooftop. Together they crashed through one . . . two . . . three fabric awnings, before bouncing off a fourth and landing in a pile of straw.

"Whew!" exclaimed Aladdin. "I haven't done that in a while."

Jasmine pulled Aladdin to his feet. "Come on. We're almost there!"

They dashed through the parade crowd. Jasmine ran past snake charmers and elephants, peacocks and fire-eaters, straight to the tigers. Just as Rajah was being loaded into a cage, Jasmine ran up and threw her arms around him.

"Rajah!" she cried. "I was so worried about you!"

Rajah rumbled happily, grateful to be rescued. Jasmine quickly removed his collar. "Come on, let's go home."

Just as she started to lead him away, a deep voice stopped her. "Where do you think you're taking my tiger?"

The parade master stood in front of Jasmine, his hands on his hips. Jasmine straightened up. "There's been a mistake," she said. "I am Princess Jasmine, and this is my tiger."

The parade master didn't believe her. "But he isn't wearing the royal collar," he pointed out.

Jasmine knew she had to prove Rajah was hers. If not, she would lose him forever! Then she had an idea.

Jasmine quickly borrowed three pieces of fruit from one of the parade members. She tossed a melon to Rajah, who balanced it on his nose.

"Princess," the parade master said slowly, "all my tigers can do that."

Jasmine tossed apples to Rajah. He balanced them on top of the melon.

The parade master wasn't convinced. "It looks as if one of my tigers is more talented than I knew!"

"But *this* is not your tiger," Jasmine said. She nodded to Rajah. Instantly, the tiger shook the fruit off and sliced it with his claws.

A chunk of melon landed at the parade master's feet. He stared at it for a moment. Then his eyes went to Rajah. "Ah," he said. "It seems I was mistaken."

"Wow! That was incredible!" a few people standing nearby exclaimed. "You should be in our parade!"

"Join the parade?" Jasmine asked, confused. "But I thought you were going to the next city tonight?"

The parade master bowed deeply. "As an apology for the mistake, Princess, we will stay in Agrabah an extra day. And we'll even perform a special show tonight in the city center. You and your tiger shall be the stars!"

That evening, everyone cheered as Rajah and Jasmine performed their special trick. Jasmine was so proud that Rajah had gotten a chance to shine. But more important, she was glad to have her friend back, right where he belonged.

Princess in Disguise

Cinderella's life had changed overnight! One day, she was cleaning and cooking for her stepmother and stepsisters. The next day, she was married to the Prince and living in a palace.

Cinderella loved living there, but sometimes, it felt strange to have the royal staff waiting on her. She often wanted to help. In the morning, she would make her own bed before the maids came in.

In the afternoon, she would sometimes invite her maids to join her for tea.

Most of all, Cinderella wanted to get to know the royal staff better. She remembered how lonely she'd been at her stepmother's house. She hoped the maids knew that she was their friend. But whenever Cinderella tried to chat with them, they would politely smile and hurry away to finish other chores.

One morning at breakfast, Cinderella told the Prince that she was worried. "I want to make sure the servants are happy working here," she said. "But I can't seem to get any of them to talk to me."

"Wouldn't they tell us if something was wrong?" the Prince asked.

Cinderella nodded. "I suppose so. I just wish there was a way to know for certain."

Later that morning, Cinderella talked with her mouse friends Jaq and Gus. “There must be something I can do to find out if the staff is happy,” she said. “But no one is going to tell me what they really think.”

“They would-a talked to you before,” Jaq said. “Cinderelly didn’t look-a like a princess then.”

Suddenly, Cinderella’s eyes lit up. “You’ve just given me an idea!” she exclaimed. “Thank you, Jaq!”

First, she went to the costume closet and found a wig. Then, she headed straight to the maids’ quarters. Luckily, no one was there. A few minutes later, Cinderella came out dressed as a member of the royal staff!

Cinderella walked down the hallway. She hoped no one would recognize her. She hadn't lived in the castle very long, so many of the servants hadn't met her yet. A moment later, she came upon a maid carrying a heavy tub of water.

"Are you new to the castle?" the maid asked when she saw Cinderella. "I don't remember meeting you before."

"Actually, I am," Cinderella answered with a smile. She helped the maid carry the large tub to the center of the ballroom. "Do you like working here?" Cinderella asked.

"Well, yes," the maid said. She thought for a moment. "But there are some things I would change."

"Like what?" Cinderella asked.

"Like this tub," the maid replied. "If only it were on wheels!"

"Why don't you suggest it?" Cinderella said.

"Oh, the royal family is very busy," the maid said. "I wouldn't want to bother them."

Next, Cinderella headed over to the banquet hall. Some of the royal staff members were at a long table. They chatted happily as they polished the silver.

"Come join us!" one of the maids called.

Cinderella walked over and examined the gleaming silver. "This looks like it's been polished already," she said.

"It was, just yesterday," the maid replied. "But we're supposed to polish it every day. Rules are rules."

Just then, Cinderella heard a voice coming from down the hall. It was Prudence, the head of the royal household! Cinderella ducked out of sight.

"Excuse me," Prudence said, pulling aside one of the maids. "When you are finished here, I'll need you to polish the backup silver."

Hmmm, Cinderella thought. She wondered if the royal family even knew they *had* backup silver. Or that it got polished so often.

When the polishing was finally finished, Cinderella went to the palace's sewing room. She had not met the seamstresses yet. What would they have to say?

When Cinderella entered the room, one of the seamstresses smiled. "Thank goodness Miss Prudence sent some extra help!" she exclaimed. "We have to finish all these gowns for the ball on Saturday."

"They're beautiful," Cinderella said, admiring the dresses.

"Gowns are my favorite things to sew," another seamstress chimed in. "Each time I finish one, I imagine what it would be like to wear it. Just once I wish we could go to a ball. I would dance and dance all night long." She sighed.

"What I wish," added another seamstress, "is that we had more light in here. I can barely see the lace I'm stitching!"

Cinderella nodded. With just a few changes, it would be easy to make these wishes come true!

Soon, it was time for lunch. Cinderella followed the maids to the kitchen. She was delighted to see steaming bowls of soup and big slices of crusty bread laid out on a long table.

But just as everyone sat down, a bell rang. The signal meant that one of the royal staff members was needed for a task. A butler at the end of the table got up. He hadn't even had a chance to taste his soup.

How silly! thought Cinderella. I'm sure it would be easy to plan chores around the staff meals. Prudence must have known she was interrupting lunch when she rang the bell.

Cinderella slipped away from the kitchen to think. She thought of the maid with her tub of water. She thought of the silver that was polished every day, and the dark sewing room.

The servants were happy working at the palace, but with a few small changes, they could be even happier. And she knew just the way to make that happen! Cinderella smiled. She had some work to do herself!

Quickly, Cinderella went to change back into her own clothes. But before she could, she bumped into the Prince.

The Prince didn't recognize her at first. But then his eyes grew wide. "Cinderella!" he exclaimed in surprise. "Why ever are you dressed like that?"

Cinderella smiled and told him the whole story. "I realized that the only way to make sure the staff was happy was to dress up as a maid myself!" she explained. "Fortunately, they didn't recognize me, and they shared the most wonderful ideas about things that would be so easy to change. Let's go see the King and the Grand Duke. I have so much to tell you all!"

Cinderella changed and then they went to see the King and the Grand Duke.

"I had quite an adventure today," Cinderella told them. "I worked alongside the royal staff. And I got some ideas for small changes that would make a big difference."

"What did you have in mind?" the King asked, curious.

"Well, changing what they work on, for a start," Cinderella replied. "I think they do the same job over and over when they could be doing other jobs that the royal family would truly appreciate. And it would be more interesting for them."

The King nodded thoughtfully. "What a grand idea!" he exclaimed. "What else do you suggest?"

That afternoon, Cinderella asked Prudence to gather the royal staff together. “It’s nice to see you all again,” Cinderella said.

Everyone was confused. No one remembered seeing her earlier that day.

Cinderella held up her disguise. “I was wearing this,” she explained. “And I worked alongside you. After hearing what you had to say, we’re going to make some changes.”

The servants looked at one another nervously.

“From now on,” Cinderella said, “all the washtubs will be on wheels, the silver will only be polished when it needs to be, more windows will be added to the sewing room, and your meals will no longer be interrupted.”

The royal staff was astonished!

“Oh, and you are all invited to the royal ball on Saturday night.” Cinderella smiled. “Does anyone have anything to add?”

“Yes, Princess,” a butler said. “Miss Prudence has fainted!”

That Saturday night, Cinderella and the Prince greeted each of the royal staff members by name as they entered the ballroom. Cinderella thanked the seamstresses for the beautiful dress they had sewn for her, the cooks for the delicious food, and the maids for making the castle sparkling clean.

The servants smiled happily as they joined in the dancing. They were growing quite fond of their new princess!

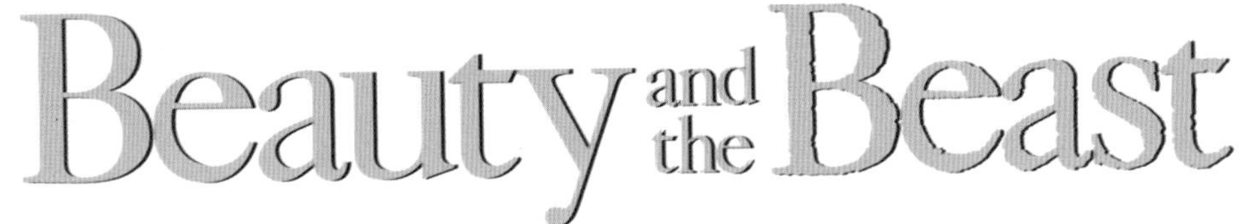

Belle Takes Charge

Belle never tired of the Beast's marvelous library. It was her favorite room in the whole castle. She knew that she could find any book her heart desired there.

Reaching the books could be a bit tricky, though. The shelves rose all the way to the ceiling. Even with the library ladder, Belle still couldn't reach the higher shelves.

One day, the Beast saw her struggling and offered to get a book she wanted.

"Oh, thank you!" Belle exclaimed. "It's that large history book. Can you reach it for me?"

The Beast climbed up. He had almost reached the book, when suddenly he heard a sharp *C-R-R-RACK!*

HISTORY

The Beast was too heavy for the ladder. It broke apart! *THUMP!* He landed on the floor.

"Are you all right?" Belle asked as she knelt by his side.

The Beast grumbled. The splintered ladder was useless now.

"It's okay," Belle told him. "We can build a new one."

"No, we cannot!" the Beast snapped. He knew his hands were too big and clumsy to handle most tools. "Just leave it!" he muttered, storming off.

But Belle wasn't used to leaving things broken. Her father was an inventor, and she was sure she could figure out a way to build a new ladder. She turned to Chip. "How would you like to help me surprise the Beast with a ladder that's as good as new?"

The teacup grinned. "I'd like that a lot! Where do we start?"

"Right here!" Belle winked. She pulled a big book about woodworking off a shelf. "With so many books, I'll bet we can learn to fix lots of things!"

According to the book, Belle and Chip needed lumber, a saw, a hammer, and some nails to build a ladder. Luckily, there was plenty of wood and a box full of tools in the barn.

Belle changed into a work dress. With Chip's help, she measured and sawed and nailed until she had built a ladder that was even sturdier and taller than the last one.

"Just wait till the Beast sees this!" Belle exclaimed.

"You made that?" the Beast asked when Belle showed everyone the ladder. He was surprised, but he still seemed a little grumpy.

"C'est magnifique!" exclaimed the candelabra, Lumiere.

"Yes, it's excellent craftsmanship!" Cogsworth the mantel clock declared.

Mrs. Potts the teapot hopped forward. "I don't suppose you know how to fix a leaky faucet, too?" she asked Belle. "The one in the kitchen has a terrible drip."

"Ah, but yes!" said Lumiere, brightening. "There is also the fireplace. Her chimney makes so much smoke!"

"A-hem!" Cogsworth jumped forward. "May I remind you that the service bell in the butler's pantry hasn't worked for a month? I think we can all agree that Belle should repair that first."

The Beast frowned. "Don't be silly," he huffed. "She's not a blacksmith or a plumber or a chimney sweep."

Belle just smiled and led her friends back to the library. "I have a feeling that with the right book, we can fix anything," she said.

To Cogsworth's delight, Belle went to the pantry first. The clock watched eagerly as she examined the broken bell on the wall. A cord that ran up to the Beast's room was attached to it. If he needed something, he could ring. But the bell seemed to be stuck.

Belle found a home-repair book that had a section on fixing hinges and read the instructions.

"Why, it just needs to be oiled," she said. She poured a few drops of oil on the bell. Then she gave it a tap.

Ding-a-ling! the bell rang.

Cogsworth jumped up and down. "Fantastic!" he exclaimed. "It's as good as new!"

Next came the chimney. According to the book Belle found, the smokestack needed to be swept clean. But that meant climbing out onto the roof.

"Be careful, Belle!" Lumiere called to her.

"Don't worry," she told her friends. "I'm doing everything by the book."

She used the brush to sweep the chimney until she had removed every bit of soot.

Once the chimney was clean, Belle went to fix the leaky faucet. She opened the repair book to the chapter on plumbing. "It says we should tighten the pipe with a wrench," she explained.

Belle twisted the wrench as hard as she could, but the joint wouldn't budge. She sighed.

Suddenly, the Beast spoke up. "Um . . . maybe I should try?"

"Of course!" Belle smiled gratefully.

With one mighty twist, the Beast fixed the leak.

"Look at that!" cried Mrs. Potts. "You two stopped the drip!"

To celebrate, Mrs. Potts made tea. Lumiere proposed a toast. "To Belle!" he said.

"And books!" Chip added.

"Hip, hip, hooray!" Cogsworth cheered.

Belle grinned. "I knew we'd find all our answers in the library," she told her friends.

"You were absolutely right," the Beast said, patting Belle's hand. "You were able to fix everything, just like you said. Thank you."

Belle went to bed that night feeling very proud—and very tired. Just as she was about to blow out her candle, she heard a light tap on her door. It was Chip.

"Hello," Belle said, surprised. "Why aren't you in bed?"

"I couldn't sleep," Chip said. "My music box stopped working. I always listen to it before bed. Can you fix it?"

"Of course." Belle smiled. But first she would have to find the right book. They tiptoed to the library and searched for a book that described how to fix music boxes. They looked and looked.

"I'm sorry, Chip," Belle said at last. "It doesn't look like there is one."

"Does that mean you can't fix it?" Chip sniffled.

"No," Belle said. "I'm sure we'll figure something out, just not tonight."

That made Chip feel a little better. "But how will I go to sleep now?" he asked.

Belle smiled. "I think I can find another book to help you."

They went back to the library, and Belle chose a storybook. Then she settled into a comfy chair with Chip in her lap. She opened the cover and began to read softly. "Once upon a time, in a faraway land . . ."

Soon, Chip's eyelids were drooping. Belle quietly closed the book and carried him back to his cupboard. She had been right. There was nothing a book—and a friend—couldn't fix.

Cooking Up a Plan

Ever since she was a little girl, Tiana loved to cook. Her father taught her everything she knew. They spent many happy hours side by side at the stove, mixing up pots of gumbo and dreaming of the restaurant they would open someday. They wanted it to be a welcoming place where all different kinds of people could come together to share food and friendship.

By the time Tiana had grown up, her father had passed away. But she still dreamed of opening the restaurant. She had her eye on an old sugar mill. It would be the perfect place!

Tiana knew it would take a lot of hard work. She got a job waiting tables at Cal's Diner and saved every penny of her tip money. Even so, she sometimes thought she might never earn enough money to buy the mill.

One day, Tiana decided to look for a second job. She figured if she worked twice as hard, she could earn the money she needed twice as fast!

Her first stop on the job hunt was Mrs. Johnson's dress shop.

"Hello?" Tiana called out from the doorway.

"Down here, dear!" replied Mrs. Johnson. The woman was sewing a hem on a gown. "Help me up, won't you?"

After Mrs. Johnson was seated, Tiana offered to finish sewing the hem. She quickly grabbed a needle and thread and began stitching.

"You have your mother's gift," Mrs. Johnson said.

"I'm glad you think so," replied Tiana, "because I was hoping to come work for you."

"Unfortunately, I'm not all that busy right now," Mrs. Johnson said. "But business usually picks up around Mardi Gras. Why don't you check back then?"

Tiana was disappointed, but she wasn't going to give up. She went to the hardware store next. Mr. Lamoreaux, the owner, greeted her cheerfully. "What can I get for you today?" he asked. "A ladder? A broom?"

"Well, I'm pretty handy," Tiana said, eyeing a sign above the counter that had come loose. She quickly grabbed a hammer and a step stool and nailed the sign back into place. "How about a part-time job?" she asked with a smile.

"I'm sorry, Tiana. I just hired my nephew," he replied. "But don't worry. Something is bound to turn up."

Back outside, Tiana noticed a steady stream of customers walking into Cora's Beauty Parlor. Maybe I'll have some luck there, she thought.

"Why don't you show me what you can do with Mrs. Richmond's hair?" Cora offered when Tiana asked for a job.

Tiana immediately set to work with curlers and hairpins. When she was done, it looked more like a wedding cake than a hairdo.

"Oh, dear. I guess I was thinking about that new dessert recipe I came up with this morning," Tiana explained. "Thank you, anyway, Cora."

Tiana's spirits were drooping as she made her way over to Duke's Café and plopped herself onto a stool. She needed to take a break.

"What's the matter?" asked Buford, the head cook. "You look down in the dumps."

"Buford, I need a job," Tiana said. Then she had a thought. "Could *you* use a new waitress? I promise I'll work hard if you give me a chance."

"I believe you," said Buford. "But we don't need anybody right now. Chin up. You'll find something." He opened the glass door on the dessert stand in front of him. "Have one of my world-famous doughnuts. I guarantee it will put a smile on your face!"

Tiana bit into the doughnut. It was dry and tasteless. But she didn't want to hurt Buford's feelings. "Thank you," she said, forcing a grin. "That certainly was . . . unlike any doughnut I've had before!"

Specials
Jambalaya
Red Beans and Rice

Back at home, Tiana told her mother, Eudora, about her disappointing day. "At this rate, I don't know if I'll ever be able to save up the money I need." Tiana sighed.

"You're already working hard enough with just one job," Eudora insisted. "Why, you don't even have time to do the things you love anymore—like cook! I sure do miss those beignets of yours. I swear they're like magic on a plate."

Suddenly, Tiana perked up. "Well, I don't know about magic . . . but they're worth a try!" she said.

"What do you mean?" Eudora asked.

"You'll see, Mama," replied Tiana.

The next morning, Tiana went to work mixing up a batch of dough. When it was done, she set it in a bowl to rise. Next, she cut the dough into squares that she dropped into a deep fryer. Soon, they turned crispy and golden.

One by one, Tiana carefully removed the beignets from the fryer and began dusting them with powdered sugar.

She smiled as she set aside one for her mother. She piled the rest onto a large plate.

Tiana walked straight over to Duke's and made a big show of putting the towering platter of beignets on the counter.

"Mmmm. Something sure does smell good," remarked a customer as the scent of beignets wafted through the café.

"What's all this?" Buford asked, interested.

"My homemade beignets," replied Tiana. "They're for being so nice to me yesterday. Go on, try one."

Buford picked up a beignet and bit into it.

"So . . . what do you think?" asked Tiana.

Buford thought the beignet was delicious. But he didn't want to admit it in a room full of his customers. After all, he was the head cook at Duke's! Still, those beignets *were* very tasty.

"Let me try another one," he said, stuffing three into his mouth at once.

"Yes?" Tiana asked.

"Hang on," Buford replied. "I don't want to be too hasty." He helped himself to another beignet . . . and another . . . and another, until half of them were gone.

"Not bad, I guess," he said finally, licking the powdered sugar off his fingers.

By now everyone was eyeing the pastries.

"Mind if I try one?" one of the customers asked.

"Me too," said another.

In no time at all, the beignets were gone, and the customers were upset.

"It's okay, Buford," Tiana said as she headed out the door. "I'll whip up another batch and come back tomorrow."

The next morning, a crowd was waiting at Buford's.

Moments later, Tiana arrived with a huge tray of the treats. The hungry customers followed her eagerly into the café.

"Say," Buford said, "could you teach me to make those?"

"Sorry, Buford," Tiana replied as she handed out the last pastry. "It's a secret family recipe. Well, I'd better be going now. I've got more job-hunting to do!"

The next morning, even more people flocked to Duke's. Buford was relieved when Tiana came through the door.

"Tiana!" he cried. "Did you bring any beignets?"

"I sure didn't," she replied.

"But that's what these folks are here for!" wailed Buford.

"It seems to me," Tiana began, "that what you need is a beignet cook *and* a waitress to help with all these extra customers. Lucky for you, I'm both rolled into one!"

"But I can't afford to offer you even one job, let alone *two*!" exclaimed Buford.

"You mean *couldn't* afford," Tiana corrected him. "My beignets have at least tripled your business. So, what do you say?"

Buford handed her an apron. "Miss Tiana," he said, "you drive a hard bargain. But you've got yourself a deal."

In no time at all, Tiana whipped up enough beignets for the whole café to enjoy.

Later that day, Tiana told her mother about her new job. "When you called my beignets 'magic on a plate,'" she explained, "I decided to let them cast their spell."

"There was no magic to it," Eudora said. "What got you that job was smarts and determination. I'm proud of you, sweetheart."

"Thanks, Mama," Tiana answered happily. She was one step closer to making her dreams come true. She took a plate from behind her back. "I made some beignets just for you. Shall we have some to celebrate?"

"I thought you'd never ask!" Eudora declared.

The Perfect Team

One morning, Prince Phillip and Princess Aurora decided to go for a ride. When they got to the royal stable, Aurora looked around. There were so many horses! And they were all so pretty! She didn't know which one to choose.

Then Aurora had an idea. "From now on, I think I'd like to ride the same horse every day," she said.

A big palomino horse caught Aurora's eye. He looked strong and handsome.

The groom brought the horse out to the ring and put him through his paces. The horse marched around as confidently as if he were the king himself. He was amazing!

Then Aurora rode him, and she liked the horse even more. "What's his name?" she asked the groom.

"We call him Brutus, Your Highness," the groom replied.

That would not do! "Brutus" sounded fierce and mean. So Aurora gave her horse a new name that was as nice as he was: Buttercup.

Aurora rode Buttercup all around the castle grounds. When a carriage rumbled past, he stood at attention. When Aurora asked him to jump a stone wall, he cleared it effortlessly. Aurora was thrilled. She had found the perfect horse!

The next day, Aurora decided to ride Buttercup out to the fairies' cottage so they could meet him. Phillip wanted to saddle up his horse, Samson, and join her. He didn't like her riding through the woods alone.

Aurora shook her head. "Don't be silly," she said. "I grew up in these woods. Besides, I won't be alone. I'll be with Buttercup. We'll take care of each other!"

Phillip knew Aurora was right. He waved good-bye as Aurora and Buttercup trotted off.

As Buttercup made his way along the smooth path near the castle, he was confident and brave. But the moment they entered the woods, he became a different horse. His steps slowed to a crawl. He looked nervous. When some of Aurora's woodland friends appeared, Buttercup tried to spin around and run away!

"There's nothing to be frightened of," Aurora said gently, trying to calm her nervous horse.

Buttercup didn't listen. When they came to a fallen log on the trail, Buttercup refused to step over it. And when Aurora asked him to walk through a forest stream, he snorted and shivered.

By the time she reached the fairies' cottage, Aurora was very worried. How could a horse who was so brave at the palace be so timid in the woods?

Flora, Fauna, and Merryweather oohed and aahed when they saw Aurora's new horse. "He's beautiful, dear," Fauna said.

Aurora sighed. Buttercup *was* beautiful. "I just wish he weren't so afraid," she said sadly.

"I'm sure it will be all right," Flora said, smiling. "You'll just need to be patient with him, that's all."

Merryweather moved closer to get a better look at Buttercup. "What a nice coat he has!" she said. "Though he might look even nicer if his hooves were blue."

She aimed her wand. *Zap!* Just like that, Buttercup's hooves turned blue.

"Don't be silly!" Flora exclaimed. "A horse shouldn't have blue hooves. On the other hand, his coat might look prettier in pink."

Zap! Zap! Zap! Back and forth the fairies went, changing Buttercup from blue to pink to green until it was hard to tell *what* color he was!

As Aurora watched her new horse change colors, she sighed. *That* didn't seem to frighten him, but a stray leaf fluttering down was as scary as a horse-eating dragon.

Suddenly, Aurora sat up. That's it! she realized. As a palace horse, Buttercup was used to people, carriages, and smooth paths. But he had never been deep in the forest before! He wasn't used to other animals, thick branches, rivers, and new noises. No wonder everything scared him!

Aurora didn't want to give up on Buttercup. She decided to help him get over his fear. But first she had to get him back to the castle.

Aurora said good-bye to the fairies and began heading home. She did her best to ignore the way Buttercup jumped at every noise. Helping him be brave was going to be hard. How would she teach him?

Just then, Buttercup stopped so suddenly that Aurora almost fell off. When she looked at the trail ahead, she gasped in horror. An enormous mountain lion was blocking their path!

They were in trouble!

If Buttercup could be scared of a bunny rabbit, he was certain to go crazy over a mountain lion!

To Aurora's surprise, Buttercup didn't panic. She could tell that he was still scared, but he stood proudly and puffed himself up. Taking a step forward, he snorted angrily. Then, Buttercup struck out at the mountain lion with his front hooves.

Aurora hung on. She was still afraid, but Buttercup had made her feel brave, too. Reaching out, she grabbed a sturdy branch from a nearby tree.

"Leave us alone!" she yelled at the mountain lion, waving the branch. "Or else!"

Buttercup pawed at the ground and snorted fiercely again.

When the mountain lion didn't budge, Buttercup leaped forward and pinned its tail to the ground with one hoof. Then Aurora rapped the mountain lion smartly on the nose with her branch.

The lion didn't like that at all. It let out an embarrassed yowl, then yanked its tail free and raced away into the woods.

Aurora was pleased with herself—and her horse. Buttercup had been brave when it counted the most.

"Come on, Buttercup," she said, giving him a pat. "Let's go home."

The horse held up his head proudly and pranced off.

As the pair neared the edge of the forest, a butterfly fluttered past. Buttercup's eyes went wide, and he jumped in terror.

But this time, Aurora just smiled. "You helped me feel brave," she said. "Now I want to help you get past your fear of the forest."

She gently stroked the horse's neck and talked to him in a soft voice. The butterfly fluttered closer and closer . . . and finally landed right on Buttercup's nose.

As the butterfly flapped its wings, Buttercup hardly shook at all.

Aurora smiled proudly. The fairies had been right. All she needed was a little patience, understanding, and trust.

"Good boy!" she praised her horse. "You know, Buttercup, I think we really do make a perfect team!"

The Quest for the Purple Pearl

"Waaaaaah!" a voice wailed in the dressing room of King Triton's underwater castle. Swimming by, Ariel stopped short. She knew that voice. It was her sister Adella, and she sounded upset!

Ariel swam closer and peeked into the room. Adella wasn't alone. Aquata, another sister, was with her.

"You can't let anyone see you. You have a bad case of the Bubbles!" Aquata was saying to Adella. "It's from eating too much sugared seaweed."

"The Bubbles?" Adella asked. She turned, and Ariel gasped.

Adella's face was covered with pink and green polka dots!

"Daddy warned me not to eat too much seaweed," Adella said. "If he sees me like this, I'll be in so much trouble!" She hiccuped, and pink and green bubbles floated up.

Aquata frowned. "Bubbles are serious. There is a cure, but it's almost impossible to find—pearl lotion made from a purple pearl. They grow inside triple-banded sea oysters."

Adella whimpered. "Don't those oysters . . . eat merfolk?"

"Sometimes," Aquata admitted.

Ariel bit her lip. Poor Adella! She needed help!

Later, in her treasure grotto, Ariel told Flounder she was going to find a purple pearl.

"You're going to do what?" Flounder exclaimed. "But the only place to get one is from a triple-banded sea oyster. And they live in Blackbeard's Trench! That means you'll have to cross the Barbed Sea Kelp Forest."

Ariel shrugged. "Adella needs help. I can't tell them I'm going because they'd worry. But someone has to get the cure. Besides, I've been in kelp forests before."

"Not like this one," Flounder said. "This kelp is huge!" He spun in a circle. "There's a riptide! Each strand of sea kelp is covered in thorns! And the spaces in between them are tiny!"

"Don't be such a guppy," Ariel said. She swung her collecting sack over her shoulder. "Are you coming?"

Flounder didn't like being called a guppy. So together, he and Ariel headed off to find the purple pearl.

The ocean path leading to the kelp forest was dark . . . and very quiet. Even though Ariel had told Flounder not to be afraid, she started to get cold fins herself as they swam along.

Up ahead was the Barbed Sea Kelp Forest. Ariel gulped. Everything Flounder had said was true. A wild riptide raced through the kelp. The spaces between the strands were barely wide enough for a small mermaid like her to fit through. But the worst part was the thorns. Each one was six inches long!

Even though she was scared, Ariel thought about Adella's polka-dotted face. She had to help her sister! With a flip of her fins, she entered the kelp forest. Carefully, she slid between two strands.

There, that wasn't so bad! She wove between three more strands. No thorns touched her. She could do this!

"Let me go ahead," Flounder said, trying to be brave. "I'm smaller than you."

"Good thinking!" Ariel said. She followed his blue tail.

Was it her imagination, or were the strands now even closer together?

"This way!" Flounder called. Ariel swam after him. A thorn scratched her arm.

Flounder zipped through another gap. But it was too tight for Ariel. "Flounder, I can't get through!" she cried.

His little face appeared in the gap. "I'll help." He held the kelp aside with his mouth. *"Mmmmmbetttrr?"*

But there still wasn't enough space. Ariel felt the pull of the riptide behind her. The current was growing stronger.

As Ariel watched, the riptide forced the kelp strands apart. This gave her an idea. What if she rode the riptide, like a dolphin in the surf, past the thorns?

"Watch out, Flounder!" she cried. "I'm coming through!"

At just the right moment, Ariel launched herself into the rushing water. The current carried her straight through a gap in the kelp. Not a single thorn scratched her!

On the other side, Ariel tumbled head over tail before grabbing on to the anchor of a shipwreck to stop herself.

She pushed the hair out of her eyes. "That was fun!" she cried.

They didn't have time to waste. Ariel needed to get that pearl and get back to her sister.

The pair swam until a giant crack split the seabed in front of them. "Blackbeard's Trench," Flounder whispered.

Ariel inched up to the edge and peered down. Far below her, the trench was lit by what looked like a golden glow.

"Here goes!" Ariel said, taking a deep breath.

They swam deeper . . . and deeper . . . and deeper.

Finally, they reached the very bottom of Blackbeard's Trench. All around them, triple-banded sea oysters were scattered like flowers in a strange underwater garden. Their shells were open, and nestled inside each one was a shimmering, glowing pearl!

"They don't *look* very scary, do they, Ariel?" Flounder asked.

Ariel shook her head. In fact, the triple-banded sea oysters were some of the prettiest creatures she'd ever seen. It was hard to believe they would ever eat a mermaid. "Maybe it's just a myth," Ariel said. "I'll just swim in and—"

"No!" Flounder grabbed Ariel's tail and pulled her back. "We've got to be sure." He took a branch of driftwood in his mouth and tossed it into the closest oyster's shell.

SNAP! The shell chomped the driftwood in half!

Ariel sighed. How was she going to get one of the pearls to cure her sister without getting hurt?

Maybe there was something in her collecting sack that could help. She emptied it out. Inside she found a dinglehopper, two gizmos, and a snarfblatt. Tucked in a corner of the bag was a long feather with a pointy tip. Her friend Scuttle had called it a mimbledoodle.

"That's no help," Flounder said. "We need a hook! Or a long rope! Or . . . something!"

But a gleam had come into Ariel's eyes. She picked up the feather. "Don't be so sure!" she said.

Ariel tied the feather to the end of a stick using some seaweed. She snuck close to one of the oysters. Then she ran the feather gently across its pink inside. She braced herself for the shell to snap shut. But instead, the oyster shuddered. It shook. It went "Ah, ah, ah—"

Ariel dropped the feather and backed away.

"AH-CHOO!"

With a mighty sneeze, the purple pearl shot out of the oyster's mouth and straight into Ariel's hands!

Flounder did a backflip. "Bull's-eye!" he yelled.

"What does that mean?" Ariel asked, confused.

The fish shrugged. "I don't know. I heard Scuttle say it once."

Together, they swam up out of Blackbeard's Trench and rode the riptide back across the Barbed Sea Kelp Forest. The ocean was still dark and quiet, but the glow from the purple pearl lit their way.

"Adella! Adella! I got it!" Ariel called as she swam into the mermaids' dressing room. Adella and Aquata were brushing their hair in front of mirrors.

"Got what, dear?" Adella asked. She turned around and . . .

Adella's face was completely clear!

"You're cured!" Ariel exclaimed. "But how? I overheard you and Aquata talking about how Bubbles—"

Aquata laughed. "Oh, Bubbles go away on their own," she said with a wave of her hand. "I was just pulling Adella's fin with that story about the purple-pearl lotion. You didn't believe it, too, did you?"

Flounder's jaw dropped.

But Ariel quickly smiled. "Oh—me? Believe that story? Of course not!"

She hid her glowing collecting bag behind her back and quickly swam out of the room.

Later, Ariel slid the beautiful pearl out of the collecting sack. It shimmered brightly.

She winked at Flounder. "It would have been a shame to turn it into lotion anyway," she said. "And I know a much better place for it than in a bottle."

Flounder grinned. That meant there was going to be a very special addition to Ariel's treasure grotto!

A Windy Adventure

Snow White was visiting the Seven Dwarfs in their forest cottage. She woke up one windy morning to the sound of leaves blowing around outside her window.

After a delicious breakfast, the Seven Dwarfs marched off to work in the mines. Snow White decided to clean up the cottage. She swept the floors and washed the dishes. Her woodland friends, an owl, a beaver, and a turtle, helped. Then she opened the cupboards.

"Potatoes, potatoes, potatoes!" She sighed. "If only there were something different to eat." Suddenly, she had an idea. "I know! I'll pick some fresh berries and nuts in the forest and bake a gooseberry-nut pie!"

The owl, beaver, and turtle nodded excitedly. They thought that was a great idea!

The owl helped Snow White fasten her cape around her neck. Then, together, they set off.

As Snow White and her animal friends walked into the forest, the wind whistled through the trees. It tangled Snow White's hair and made her cheeks turn pink. But she didn't mind. With all the juicy berries and fallen nuts they were collecting, she would be able to make a lovely pie that evening!

Before long, she came to a fork in the trail.

"I've never taken the trail on the right before," she said, pointing to the long, shady path.

"It would be nice to go exploring," Snow White continued. "I'm sure there are nuts and berries along that path, too."

Snow White looked down the trail. Not too far off, a wooden bridge swayed above a river. Just then, a gust of wind blew her toward the new path. She laughed. "I think that's a sign, don't you?" she asked her friends.

They headed down the trail and across the rickety wooden bridge.

On the other side of the bridge, the path curved. Snow White was sure it led somewhere special!

The trail wound left and then right before opening into a sunlit grove. The clearing was filled with nut trees!

"How wonderful!" Snow White exclaimed. She dashed from one to the other. There were walnut trees, chestnut trees, and almond trees. The grove even had a cluster of gooseberry bushes!

"Now, you pick the nuts from the high branches," she told the owl. He saluted with one wing and flew to the very top of a tree.

"And you gather the ones on the ground," she said to the beaver. The little animal shook his tail and scampered off.

"And you—" Snow White turned to the turtle. But he wasn't there. She laughed. It always took the turtle a little longer to catch up. "That's okay. I'll take care of the berries."

Snow White and her friends got to work. The wind whistled through the branches as Snow White filled her basket.

Suddenly, a mighty gust snatched Snow White's cape right off her shoulders.

"Oh, dear!" she cried. She got up and began to chase her cape through the woods.

The wind carried it down a pebbled path and past a large rock. It flew farther and farther away.

Finally, the cape snagged on a tree branch. Snow White untangled it. But when she turned around, she realized that she was lost.

For a moment, Snow White was frightened. Then she put her hands on her hips. "I'll just have to find my way back on my own," she said.

Snow White looked around. Which way had she come from? The left or the right? Then she glanced at her feet. Her slippers were muddy. She'd left footprints in the dirt. "I can follow my own tracks!" she exclaimed.

Snow White carefully followed her own trail of footprints. Soon, the ground changed from dirt to pebbles. There weren't any footprints here. Now which way should I go? she wondered. Suddenly, she noticed a large rock up ahead. "I passed that when I chased my cape!" she exclaimed.

Snow White hurried toward the rock. Once she was there, she could see the grove in the distance. "Owl! Beaver!" she called.

Hearing her voice, the owl flew from the top of a walnut tree, and the beaver scampered out to meet her. They both looked very relieved.

"I had such an adventure!" Snow White told them, picking up her basket. Then she looked around. "Oh, my, is Turtle not here yet?" she asked.

"What if he got lost the same way I did? We had better go and find him."

Snow White, Owl, and Beaver hurried back along the forest path. When they reached the river's edge, they discovered that the old bridge had broken.

"Oh, no!" Snow White cried. She could see the poor turtle. He was stranded on a rock in the middle of the water. The wind must have caused the bridge to fall—with him on it! Now there was no way for Turtle to climb the steep walls of the riverbank.

Snow White studied the ground where the bridge had been attached. The wooden stakes at one end had come loose and been swept away by the water. Now the bridge dangled from the other side of the river, its rope ends trailing in the water.

"Don't worry, little turtle!" she called. "We'll save you!"

But the water was rushing too fast for her to swim. How could she rescue the turtle and fix the bridge?

"Owl can fly over," Snow White said thoughtfully. "And Beaver is good at chewing. There must be something we can do."

Suddenly, Snow White had an idea! She snapped a stick off a nearby tree and drew a picture of the broken bridge in the dirt.

"Here's what we need to do," she explained to her friends. "Owl, if you fly to the other side and pick up the rope ends, Beaver can chew some new wooden stakes. And I can hammer them in place. Together, we can rebuild the bridge."

The three friends went to work. The beaver liked to gnaw, so chewing new stakes from tree branches was easy for him. Once he was done, Snow White hammered the stakes into the ground with a rock.

Meanwhile, the owl flew across the river and took the ends of the ropes in his beak. But the bridge was heavy, so he hooted to some of his bird friends to help him lift it out of the water. Then Snow White pulled the bridge tight and tied the ropes to the stakes.

"Good as new!" she cried. "Thank you, friends!"

Snow White quickly stepped onto the bridge. They had done such a good job, it hardly swayed at all.

When she reached the middle, she dropped to her knees. Looking over the side, Snow White saw the turtle waiting on the rock just below her. But the water was picking up speed. She needed to get him right away. Snow White stretched down as far as she could and scooped the turtle up into her arms.

She was just in time! A big gush of water washed right over the rock just as Snow White picked up the turtle.

The turtle breathed a sigh of relief. He nuzzled Snow White to thank her.

"What are friends for?" she said with a smile. "I think that's enough adventure for one day. Let's head home to bake that pie."

Together, the friends made their way back down the path. This time, they knew just where they were going.

When Snow White and her animal friends got back to the cottage, she baked a lovely gooseberry-nut pie. Just as it was coming out of the oven, the Seven Dwarfs arrived home.

"That's mighty delicious-looking," Bashful said softly.

"Did you have any troblems—prouble—uh, problems today?" Doc asked.

Snow White winked at the owl, the beaver, and the turtle. "Nothing we couldn't handle!" she replied.

A Fateful Adventure

Long ago, in the lush, green highlands of Scotland, lived a princess named Merida. She had three mischievous little brothers named Hamish, Hubert, and Harris. Her father, King Fergus, was very jolly, even though his leg had been bitten clean off by a demon bear many years ago. Merida's mum, Queen Elinor, was loving, but strict. She kept Merida very busy.

As the future queen, Merida had many responsibilities. Her days were filled with long classes and dos and don'ts.

But every once in a while, Merida had a day to herself. She would race her horse, Angus, through the forest, climb to the top of gigantic waterfalls, and shoot her trusty bow and arrow.

One evening, Merida received some very unpleasant news. The lords of the three neighboring clans were going to present their firstborn sons as her suitors. There would be a competition. The winner would be given Merida's hand in marriage.

Merida was upset. She didn't want to get married! But then she realized something. She was a firstborn, too! And it was up to *her* to pick the competition. She chose archery.

The day of the competition arrived. All the suitors lined up.

The first one missed the bull's-eye completely. The second did not do much better. The third hit the bull's-eye, but Merida wasn't worried. "I'll be shooting for my own hand!" she announced. When Merida fired at the target, her arrow split the third suitor's arrow right down the middle. She had beaten all three suitors!

The clans were very angry. Merida's mother was *furious.*

"You don't know what you've done!" Queen Elinor scolded when she and her daughter were alone. "It will be fire and sword if it's not set right!"

Merida was upset. She picked up her sword and slashed the family tapestry in two. Elinor threw Merida's prized bow into the roaring fire.

Heartbroken, Merida ran to the stable. She and Angus raced off into the forest. Suddenly, Angus stopped dead in his tracks.

Merida flew through the air, landing hard on the ground. When she stood up, she found herself inside a ring of giant stones. Then she saw strange lights that seemed to be beckoning to her. They were the mysterious will-o'-the-wisps!

Merida followed the lights to a cottage in the woods. She walked up and opened the door. Inside stood a witch!

"I want a spell to change my mum!" Merida cried. "That will change my fate!"

"Last time I did this was for a prince," the witch warned. "He demanded I give him the strength of ten men."

The witch began to toss strange things into her cauldron. There was a flash of brilliant green light. Then she pulled a small cake from the bubbling goo and gave it to Merida.

Merida went home and gave the cake to her mother. As soon as Queen Elinor took a bite, she began to feel woozy.

Merida helped Elinor up to her room and into bed. The queen tossed and turned. Then she rolled right off the bed. When she sat up, Merida screamed. The witch's spell had transformed her mother into a huge bear with large teeth and razor-sharp claws!

Merida quickly realized that her mother was in great danger. Ever since King Fergus had lost his leg, he had made it his business to hunt down any bear that crossed his path.

"If he so much as sees you, you're dead!" Merida shouted. "We've got to get out of the castle!"

Mother and daughter raced out of the castle and into the forest to find the witch and reverse the spell. They could not find her, but she had left Merida a message: "By the second sunrise, your spell will be permanent unless you remember these words: Fate be changed, look inside, mend the bond torn by pride."

Exhausted, they fell asleep. They awoke to the first sunrise and saw that the will-o'-the-wisps had appeared. The wisps led them to the remains of an ancient castle where a prince had once lived.

As Merida explored the ruins, she saw claw marks ripped into the stone. She realized something. "The spell! It's happened before!"

The castle had belonged to the very same prince that the witch had spoken of. He had asked for the strength of ten men—and she had changed him into Mor'du, the demon bear who had taken King Fergus's leg!

Just then, Mor'du attacked. Merida and Queen Elinor barely escaped.

"If we don't hurry," Merida told her mother, "you'll become like Mor'du, a bear—a *real* bear. Forever!"

Luckily, Merida had an idea of how to break the spell. "Mend the bond torn by pride," she said, thinking of the witch's words. "The tapestry!" They had to get back to the castle!

When they arrived, the queen was able to hide in plain sight. A dreadful fight was going on. The clans were upset because Merida had not chosen a suitor. Merida realized she had to step in before it was too late.

She took a deep breath and began to speak. Her mother gestured to help her figure out what to say. Merida reminded everyone of the battles they had fought together. And then she spoke of breaking tradition and letting people decide for themselves whom they would love.

To Merida's amazement, the clans—and her mother—liked her idea.

Eager to tell his wife what had happened, King Fergus headed upstairs. He thought Elinor was still sick. But to his great shock, he didn't find his queen—he discovered a bear instead. He drew his sword.

Racing into the room, Merida tried to stop her father. But Fergus would not listen. He locked Merida in her room, and then he and his men chased Elinor.

With some help from her brothers, who had eaten the witch's cake and turned into bear cubs, Merida escaped.

Grabbing the tapestry, a needle, and thread, she and her brothers rode into the forest, Merida sewing frantically all the while. She had to end the curse before the men found her mother.

The men had cornered Elinor at the Ring of Stones and tied her up. Fergus stepped forward and raised his sword over his head. Merida had to do something.

Thinking quickly, she threw herself in front of Queen Elinor. "I'll not let you kill my mother!" she shouted at King Fergus.

Just then, a huge, horrible beast stepped into the ring and let out a terrible roar. It was Mor'du! He grabbed Fergus and flung him into the stones. Then he lunged at Merida.

Seeing her daughter in danger, Elinor gathered all her strength and rose up, breaking the ropes that bound her. She shoved Mor'du away from Merida. But Elinor was no match for the demon bear. He threw her into a stone. Merida raced over to be by her mother's side.

As the demon bear came closer, Merida and Elinor clung to each other. Just as Mor'du was about to reach them, a broken stone toppled onto him. He was defeated.

Moments later, the second sun began to rise. Merida quickly placed the mended tapestry over her mother and closed her eyes.

When she opened them, Queen Elinor was still a bear. "I want you back, Mummy," Merida sobbed. "I love you." She threw her arms around Elinor's neck and nuzzled into the warm bear fur.

As Merida's words faded, she felt a hand on her head—a human hand! She looked up, right into her mother's beautiful face.

"Mum, you're back!" Merida cried. Gratefully, she touched her mother's cheek. "You changed!"

"Oh darling, we both have," Elinor said tenderly.

And it was true. Now Merida knew that the power to change her fate lived within her. She just had to be brave enough to do it.

Rapunzel's Challenge

Rapunzel skipped along happily as Flynn Rider guided her through the forest. She couldn't believe it. For eighteen years, she had watched from her tower window as magical lanterns floated up into the sky on her birthday. All her life, she had dreamed of seeing the lights up close. And now, with Flynn as her guide, Rapunzel had finally left her tower and was traveling to the kingdom. Her dream was about to come true!

Flynn, however, was not happy about the plan. He was a thief. Earlier that morning he had climbed into Rapunzel's tower looking for a place to hide. He was running away from the king's guards because he had stolen a jeweled crown.

Rapunzel had taken the crown and only agreed to give it back if Flynn took her to see the lights. So now Flynn found himself leading her into the very kingdom where he was a wanted man! If only he could talk her out of it.

Suddenly, he had an idea.

"You know, Blondie," Flynn said quite casually, "the forest can be dangerous. It's no place for someone like you."

Rapunzel frowned. "What do you mean 'someone like me'?" she asked. "Anything you can do, I can do, too. In fact, I'll bet that I can do it *better* than you!"

"Did you say 'bet'?" Flynn grinned. "Well, why don't we have a contest to see if that's true? If I win, I get back my satchel and you promise to go home."

Rapunzel shook her head. "No, the satchel can't be part of the bet. We have a deal," she pointed out. "The prize should be something else." She thought for a moment. What could the winner get? Then she looked at her chameleon friend, Pascal. He rubbed his tiny green tummy eagerly.

"Oh, I know!" Rapunzel exclaimed. She pulled out her iron skillet and pointed it at Flynn. "Whoever loses has to make the winner a snack."

"You're on, Blondie," Flynn said. He chuckled. It didn't matter. Whatever challenge they decided on, he knew he'd win.

"What kind of contest should we have?" Rapunzel asked. "A painting challenge? A game of chess?"

Flynn scoffed. "This should be a contest of survival," he said. "Remember, it's dangerous out in these woods. For example . . . " He pointed to a tall tree. "What if a wild animal were chasing us? Who could climb this tree the fastest?" He winked. "Do you think you could beat me?"

Rapunzel squared her shoulders. In a flash, she threw her long hair onto a low branch and swung gracefully up into the tree.

"Hang on!" Flynn cried, dashing after her. "I didn't say go!" He quickly pulled out two arrows and used them to climb up the tree right past Rapunzel.

This is too easy! he thought. She'll never beat me. I'm the fastest climber in the kingdom.

When he'd almost reached the top of the tree, Flynn stopped and looked down. Rapunzel was nowhere in sight. She's an even slower climber than I thought! Flynn said to himself.

Suddenly, from up above, Flynn heard a voice call down.

"Yoo-hoo! Flynn Rider! What took you so long?"

Flynn looked up and gasped. Rapunzel was sitting on the top branch of the tree. “How did you get up there so fast?” he cried.

Rapunzel pointed proudly to her golden hair. “You’d be surprised how much I can do with this,” she said. “No branch is too high for my hair to reach.”

"That's cheating," Flynn argued. "You can't use your hair to help you. I demand another contest. And this time, no hair."

Rapunzel was disappointed. She didn't like not being able to use her hair. But she didn't need it. She was having so much fun! She agreed to another contest. They decided to have a race next. Pascal would start them off.

"First one to the river wins," Flynn declared.

Pascal gave the signal, and then they were off!

Rapunzel and Flynn sprang forward from the starting line. They ran as fast as they could.

There's no way she'll win this time, Flynn thought. Her hair can't help her run.

But as Flynn raced along, he noticed a sign tacked to a tree. WANTED! it said in bold letters. BY ORDER OF THE KING. And Flynn's picture was on it! But the nose looked slightly off. . . .

"Not again!" Flynn moaned. The WANTED posters always showed him with a fat and crooked nose.

Flynn was staring so hard at the poster that Rapunzel sped right past him. Her gleaming hair trailed behind her.

I can't lose! Flynn thought. He doubled his speed . . . and accidentally tripped over Rapunzel's hair! Before he knew it, he was completely tangled in her long locks.

Rapunzel didn't realize what had happened. She kept running and sprinted to the river's edge. She had won!

She turned around and smiled. But to her surprise, she saw Flynn wrapped up in her hair.

"That wasn't fair," he panted. "You used your hair again."

"No, I didn't," Rapunzel argued. "I only used my legs."

But Flynn insisted they have one more contest. Rapunzel sighed, then she agreed. After all, she had beaten Flynn twice. Surely she could do it one more time.

Flynn pointed to the wide river in front of them. "Let's see who can cross this first," he said.

Uh-oh, thought Rapunzel. Because she'd never been allowed to leave her tower, she didn't know how to swim. And the river was moving fast!

As Flynn dove into the water, Rapunzel looked around. How could she get across without swimming? Or using her hair?

"Any ideas?" she asked Pascal, who was hanging from a nearby vine. The little chameleon shrugged. But then Rapunzel's eyes lit up. "That's it!" she cried.

Flynn panted as he climbed out of the river. He was dripping wet. "I did it," he said happily. "I won!" Then he looked up, and his jaw dropped.

Rapunzel was standing on the shore, as dry as she had been on the other side.

"I don't understand," Flynn sputtered. "You got here first? And you're not even wet?"

Rapunzel nodded. "That's because I didn't swim across," she said. "I swung across."

"Oh, I see," Flynn said. He shook the water from his hair and grinned slyly. "Then I win! Remember? We made a deal that you couldn't use your hair."

"I didn't use my hair," Rapunzel said. She held up a long, thick vine. It stretched back all the way back to the far side of a tall tree on the opposite side of the river. "I might have learned how to swing on my hair," she explained. "But this time, I used this!" She explained how she had swung over him.

Flynn sighed. He hated to admit it, but Rapunzel had beaten him. Again. Glumly, he poured the river water out of his boots. "Fine, you win." He sighed. "Come on, Blondie. It's on to the kingdom now, I guess."

"Wait. What about the prize?" Rapunzel reminded him. She pulled out her skillet. "You owe us a snack. And we're hungry! Aren't we, Pascal?"

"Well, what would you like?" Flynn asked Rapunzel.

"Surprise us!" Rapunzel answered excitedly.

While she and Pascal waited in the cool shade of a cherry tree, Flynn built a fire. Then he began to gather nuts and cherries and cook them. Soon, delicious smells filled the air.

"Mmm!" Rapunzel said, taking a bite. It was one of the tastiest treats she'd ever had.

"You know," Rapunzel told Flynn with a wink, "you might be almost as good at cooking as I am . . . almost."

Trouble in the Forest

"Raspberries again?" Merryweather frowned at her bowl. The fairies and Briar Rose were just sitting down to a tasty breakfast in their cottage. Of course, Briar Rose didn't know that her aunts were fairies or that she was really a princess. For sixteen years, Flora, Fauna, and Merryweather had raised Briar Rose in secret. As long as she was hidden in the forest, she was safe from the evil fairy, Maleficent. Usually, the good fairies were cheerful. But this morning, Merryweather was a bit grumpy.

"I like *blueberries,*" Merryweather complained. "Why can't we have more of those?"

"You know perfectly well why," Flora replied. "There aren't any blueberry bushes for miles."

"I could go pick blueberries," Briar Rose offered.

"Oh, no, dear," Merryweather quickly replied. The fairies never wanted Briar Rose to stray too far. Merryweather popped a red berry into her mouth. "Raspberries are just fine."

But after breakfast, Merryweather was still thinking about blueberries. Just because Briar Rose shouldn't go far doesn't mean that I can't, she said to herself. Quietly, she picked up her cloak and snuck out of the cottage.

"Where in the world is Merryweather?" Fauna asked later.

"You don't think she went off on her own to get blueberries?" Flora whispered, worried.

"Oh, no!" Fauna gasped. "The patch is so far away. What if she gets into trouble?"

Flora and Fauna decided to go look for Merryweather. They told Briar Rose to stay home in case Merryweather returned. "We won't be gone long," Flora said.

Several hours passed. Briar Rose waited . . . and waited. She began to worry. It was late afternoon, and her aunts hadn't returned. "I know they said to stay here," she said. "But this is so unlike them! I have to go make sure they're all right."

A short while later, Briar Rose was walking through the forest. Her animal friends scampered up to her. They thought she was coming to visit.

"I'm afraid I can't stay today," she told them. "I'm looking for some people."

"Who?" the owl hooted.

"My aunts," Briar Rose answered. "I think they went to find blueberries. Do you know where the blueberry bushes grow?"

The animals led Briar Rose down a shady path to a part of the forest that she'd never visited. They walked for a long time. Just when Briar Rose was beginning to wonder if they were on the right track, she spotted a bright piece of blue cloth dangling from a sharp branch.

"This came from Merryweather's cloak!" she exclaimed. "We must be on the right path!"

At last, the animals led Briar Rose to a clearing. She looked around. There were lots of blueberry bushes. But no aunts.

"Where could they be?" she asked.

Suddenly, two familiar voices called down from above.

"Briar Rose? Is that you, dear?"

Looking up, Briar Rose saw Flora and Fauna caught in a large net that was dangling from a tree branch. "Aunt Flora, Aunt Fauna!" Briar Rose cried. "What are you doing up there?"

Just then, Briar Rose heard another voice. This one was coming from the ground.

"Hello? Is anyone up there?"

"Aunt Merryweather?" Briar Rose peered over the edge of a deep hole in the ground. It was partly covered with leaves. Merryweather was at the bottom.

"You shouldn't be here! These are hunters' traps," Flora called down. "They're very dangerous."

"Don't worry, Aunt Flora," Briar Rose said. "I'll get you down." She began to climb the tree.

"Oh, no," cried Fauna. "You might hurt yourself!"

"I'll be careful," Briar Rose promised.

The fairies watched nervously as Briar Rose made her way up the tree. The limbs creaked and swayed beneath her feet. But soon, she reached the branch their net was tied to. "Now, hold on while I untie this knot," she called.

Thump! The fairies dropped down and landed on the soft grass. They were free!

Next Briar Rose had to rescue Merryweather. But the hole that Merryweather was in was very deep.

"It's no use. We can't reach her." Flora sighed.

"If only our arms were longer," Fauna added.

What her aunts said gave Briar Rose an idea. "Our arms might not be long enough. But the net is!" she exclaimed.

Quickly, Briar Rose dragged the net to the edge of the hole and tossed one end of it down. Merryweather was able to climb up it like a ladder!

The fairies smiled proudly at Briar Rose. “You rescued us all!” Merryweather exclaimed.

“But now we must hurry home, dear,” Flora said. “It’s not safe this far from the cottage.”

Kuh-lump, kuh-lump, kuh-lump! Suddenly, the sound of horses’ hooves echoed through the forest.

“Oh, no. Someone is coming!” Fauna gasped.

"It must be the hunters," said Flora. "They're coming back to check their traps."

"Really?" asked Briar Rose. She looked up curiously. The only people Briar Rose knew were her aunts. She couldn't help feeling a little excited about meeting someone new.

But Flora quickly pulled her along. "Come, child. We must hide!" she warned.

Briar Rose and the fairies quickly ducked behind the biggest, thickest blueberry bush they could find. A moment later, two hunters rode into the clearing.

"What happened to our traps?" asked the man with a thick, black beard.

"It looks like something sprung them," the other said. He picked up the empty net. "But how did it get out? Where did it go?"

They looked around the clearing for clues. Suddenly, the black-bearded hunter bent down. He picked up Merryweather's blueberry basket!

"I'll bet whoever left this set off our traps," said the black-bearded hunter. "It looks like a peasant girl's basket. I wonder where she went?"

Behind the bush, the three fairies gulped. They didn't want the hunters discovering Briar Rose. They needed to sneak away—as fast as they could!

The fairies looked at one another, worried. How could they get away without the hunters seeing them?

Just then, Briar Rose spotted her owl friend. That gave her an idea. She pointed to the men and made a flapping motion to the owl. Then she put her finger to her lips and winked. The owl understood at once. He quietly flew out over the clearing, above the hunters' heads.

"Come out, come out," the hunters called. "We know you're here. There's no need to hide."

"Who?" came the reply from the opposite side of the clearing.

"Did you hear that?" exclaimed the black-bearded hunter. He thought the owl was a person.

"It came from that way," the other said. "Let's go!"

In a flash, they were off chasing the owl. Once they were gone, Briar Rose and the fairies sneaked out from behind the bush to make their way home, safe and sound.

Back at the cottage, the fairies couldn't stop smiling at Briar Rose. "I don't know what we would have done without you," Fauna said.

"You were very brave," Flora added. "But no more sneaking off. For any of us."

Merryweather sighed. "I'm sorry," she said. "I guess it serves me right that I didn't get any blueberries."

Suddenly, Briar Rose grinned. She pulled Merryweather's basket out from behind her back. It was full of blueberries!

"After such an exciting adventure," Briar Rose said, "how could we settle for anything less than blueberries?"

A Hidden Gem

One bright summer morning, Tiana was discussing party plans with her mother and her friend Charlotte. Tiana's birthday was just days away! She was very excited. She loved birthday parties.

Nearby, Prince Naveen frowned as he listened to Tiana talk. Although he had spent weeks looking, he still hadn't found the perfect gift for his princess. And now time was running out!

Luckily, the following day, Naveen overheard Tiana speaking with Charlotte.

"When my daddy and I used to go fishing in the bayou, we'd sometimes find a piece of swamp amber," said Tiana. "I thought it was the most precious thing in all the world!"

"Swamp amber?" Charlotte asked. She had never heard of such a thing.

Tiana nodded. "Swamp amber is more beautiful than diamonds and pearls! I wish I had some to show you!"

Hidden from sight, Naveen smiled. "That's it!" he whispered as he dashed out the door. Now he knew just what to do!

First, Naveen met up with his friend Louis. He told the alligator his plan. Louis was happy to help Naveen out. After all, Tiana was one of his good friends, too. Then the two of them went to ask Mama Odie if she could help them find some swamp amber.

"You don't need my help!" said Mama Odie, laughing. "Go find it yourself. You know what to do."

Naveen was nervous. He hoped Mama Odie was right. Otherwise, he would have nothing to give his princess.

Soon, it was the day of Tiana's birthday. The chefs put the final touches on her cake while the guests began to arrive. Yet when Tiana went to get Naveen, she couldn't find him anywhere. She asked her mother and Charlotte, but they hadn't seen him either.

Finally, one of the guests said he had spotted the prince down by the old mossy tree in the bayou. Eudora and Charlotte told Tiana not to worry. But Tiana was afraid Naveen might be in trouble. She had to go help him!

Tiana ran out of her party and down to the river. She climbed into a rowboat and made her way out to the bayou.

When she arrived at the old mossy tree, she saw Naveen. He was standing on one of the tree's big roots. Louis sat on the bank, trying to get a thorn out of his foot. Tiana let out a big sigh of relief. Naveen was okay!

But then, as she watched, he dove into the water and disappeared.

"Naveen!" Tiana cried out, her heart pounding. She waited. Then she waited some more. When the prince didn't reappear, Tiana stood up in the rowboat. She removed the sashes and petticoats from her dress, took a deep breath, and dove into the water!

The water was murky and, for a moment, Tiana couldn't see anything. Then she spotted Naveen. He seemed to be caught in a tangle of roots. Tiana grabbed his hand and pulled him to the surface.

"I was so worried about you!" Tiana cried when they were safely in the rowboat. "What on earth were you doing out here in the bayou?"

Naveen looked down at his closed hand. Then he opened it to reveal a plain, muddy rock. "I'm a little embarrassed," he said. "I was expecting to find you a sparkling jewel, but this is just . . . "

"Swamp amber!" Tiana exclaimed happily. "What a wonderful birthday surprise!"

Together, they rowed out of the bayou. They needed to get back to the party. Everyone was probably wondering where they were!

When Tiana and Naveen walked in, the guests gasped at the sight of them. They were covered in mud! But Tiana didn't care. She was just happy that she had found Naveen and that he had given her such a thoughtful gift. She smiled at him.

As the prince and princess went to change their clothes, Mama Odie picked up the amber. "A little sparkle couldn't hurt," she said, and tossed the rock into a pot of gumbo.

In a puff of magic, the swamp amber became a dazzling necklace with a golden jewel.

When Tiana and Naveen returned to the party, Mama Odie showed them the swamp amber.

Tiana gasped. The amber sparkled and shone. And when the light hit it, the gem glowed like a little sun. Tiana had never seen anything so beautiful in her whole life. "How did you do that?" she asked.

Mama Odie winked at Tiana. "Oh, it's just a talent we have down in the bayou. We like to take things that are a little slimy and rough around the edges and turn them into something wonderful."

"Like turning crawfish into gumbo," Tiana said.

"Like taking sugar and spinning it into a beignet," Charlotte added.

"Or a frog into a prince!" Naveen agreed.

Tiana looked down at her swamp amber. She felt so lucky. Naveen had worked so hard to find her the perfect gift.

As she and Naveen began to dance, Tiana smiled. This had turned out to be one of the best birthdays ever!

Shark Surprise

Ariel was swimming near the ocean surface one day when she heard a *rat-a-tat-tat* above her head. Curious, she popped out of the water. Her friend Scuttle was on a rock. He was beating what looked like a musical instrument.

"Hey, Ariel! Check out my wing tapper!" the seagull called.

"Where did you get it?" Ariel asked.

"It just floated by," Scuttle replied. "It must have come from that new shipwreck out by Coral Cove."

Ariel couldn't believe her ears. A new shipwreck with musical instruments on board? She had to find it!

Ariel rushed home to get her collecting bag. As she passed the throne room, she saw her father speaking with her sisters.

"A large shark has been spotted in our waters," King Triton warned. "I want all of you to stay close to the palace today." He looked straight at Ariel. "Especially you," he said.

"Don't worry, Daddy! I won't go too far," Ariel called as she rushed off.

But King Triton wasn't convinced. He ordered Sebastian, the court composer, to follow Ariel and make sure she stayed out of trouble.

Ariel quickly found her friend Flounder. She told him about the sunken ship. "It has humans' musical objects!" she said excitedly.

"But Ariel," Flounder interrupted, "didn't you hear? There's a big shark swimming around out there."

"Oh, Flounder. We won't go far," Ariel said. "Besides, if we don't hurry, all the treasure will float away."

"Okay," Flounder finally agreed. "As long as we're quick."

Just beyond Coral Cove, Ariel spotted the shipwreck. "There it is!" she cried. She swam through a large hole in the deck. "Isn't this incredible?" she whispered. Flounder didn't answer.

"Flounder?" Ariel turned around. "Where are you?"

"Ariel, help!"

Ariel hurried back to the deck and found her friend caught in a fishing net.

"I'm stuck," Flounder said, wriggling.

Ariel held on to Flounder's fins and tugged until he popped free.

"That was close." Flounder sighed. "We should head back."

"Not yet!" Ariel insisted. "We still have to find the musical instruments." Suddenly, they heard a loud clang from inside the ship.

"What was that?" Flounder asked nervously.

"Music to my ears!" Ariel said. She and Flounder swam through the hole in the deck. Soon they discovered a large, beautiful room. It was filled with musical instruments. "Humans must have held concerts in here!" Ariel said, clapping her hands excitedly. It was even better than she'd imagined.

She swam about, collecting some of the smaller instruments. Meanwhile, Flounder ran his tail along the strings of a harp.

"Hey, Ariel!" he exclaimed. "Did you hear that? Maybe Sebastian will let me be in the orchestra."

But Ariel was busy examining a tuba. "This sure is a funny-looking thing," she said. She put her lips to it and blew as hard as she could. Out popped Sebastian!

"Sebastian!" cried Ariel. "What are you doing here?"

"Chasing after you, that's what!" Sebastian said. "You're coming home with me, young lady. This instant!"

"Ariel! Sebastian!" Flounder interrupted. "Look!" He pointed to the window.

A giant shark was staring at them from outside!

Smash! The shark crashed through the window.

Sebastian and Flounder were terrified. But Ariel thought quickly. She used her tail to knock over a large drum in front of the shark. The shark swam straight through it . . . and got stuck!

"Come on!" Ariel cried, racing out of the room with Sebastian and Flounder.

The three friends zipped through the hole in the ship's deck and into the open water. But the shark got loose and chased after them.

"Hold on tight!" Ariel yelled to Flounder and Sebastian. She grabbed her friends and began swimming in loop-de-loops and zigzags. The shark got so dizzy, he couldn't follow them.

While the shark was off balance, Ariel darted into a small cave in Coral Cove.

The friends kept very quiet. But a tambourine accidently slipped and fell out of Ariel's bag. *Clang!*

The shark heard the noise and found them.

"We're doomed!" cried Sebastian.

Ariel swam in front of her friends to protect them. But then she noticed the shark eyeing the tambourine.

"Do you like music?" she asked carefully.

The shark nodded. Ariel pulled out a few more instruments. "Just play along," she whispered to Flounder and Sebastian. Ariel began singing while Flounder tapped the tambourine and Sebastian plucked the strings on a violin.

"Bravo!" cried the shark. "I just love music. I tried to join you before. But you swam away too quickly."

"You mean you're not going to eat us?" Flounder asked.

"Oh, no," the shark replied. "I'm more interested in music than in merfolk and their friends."

The shark introduced himself. "My name is Fang," he said.

"It's nice to meet you, Fang," Ariel said. Then she had an idea. "We have an orchestra back at the palace. Do you think you'd like to join it?"

Sebastian nearly fainted!

"I wish I could," Fang said with a sigh. "But my fins are too short to play an instrument. And my voice is all scratchy."

"Well, that's that!" said Sebastian, relieved.

But Ariel shook her head. "There must be an instrument you can play." Suddenly, she noticed the shark's enormous teeth. "Or an instrument you can *be*!"

She grabbed two felt mallets from her sack. "Smile, please," she instructed. When the shark did, she played his huge teeth like a xylophone. The sound was enchanting.

"See?" Ariel grinned. "He'd make the perfect addition to your orchestra, Sebastian!"

Sebastian shook his head. "Ariel, the king will never allow a shark in the orchestra."

"Don't worry," Ariel said. "I think I know a way to convince Daddy."

Back at the palace, Fang waited outside while Ariel and her friends swam to the throne room. "Daddy," Ariel began. "What would you say if I told you we'd met an amazing musician?"

"I'd say that's wonderful," King Triton replied. "And who is this talented creature?"

"He's a shark!" Flounder blurted out as Fang swam in.

At first, King Triton did *not* want Fang in the orchestra. Then he heard the shark's special music. After Ariel explained that Fang didn't eat merfolk, King Triton finally agreed.

"I know just how to celebrate," Ariel said. "We should hold a special concert starring the orchestra's newest member!"

That weekend, all the merfolk in the kingdom swam into the concert hall to hear the shark. They were a bit nervous. But they were also very curious. Fang was nervous, too.

Sebastian raised his baton. Ariel nodded at Fang. "Let's show them what you've got!"

The shark opened his mouth in a wide smile. The audience gasped.

But when Ariel began to play Fang's teeth like a xylophone, everyone cheered and clapped. The music was wonderful!

"Thank you for making my dream come true," Fang told Ariel after the concert.

The princess laughed. "I went on an adventure to find humans' musical instruments," she said, "but I came back with the biggest musical surprise under the sea!"

Against All Odds

Princess Jasmine and Aladdin were strolling across the palace grounds one evening when the Sultan ran out onto the balcony.

"Drat!" the Sultan cried. "That dratted Desert Race!"

Every year, the best riders from Agrabah competed against the riders from the neighboring kingdom of Zagrabah. The fastest horse and rider were awarded the prized Golden Palm trophy.

Jasmine's father was upset because Prince Fayiz of Zagrabah had won it for the last three years.

"I have an idea, Father!" Jasmine said eagerly. "I could ride my horse Midnight in the Desert Race this year. He's the fastest horse in Agrabah!"

The Sultan did not like that idea. The race was dangerous, and he didn't want his only daughter hurt.

"How about if *I* ride Midnight in the race?" Aladdin suggested.

Immediately, the Sultan's face brightened. He liked *that* idea very, very much!

Aladdin had never ridden Midnight before. In fact, nobody but Jasmine had ever ridden him. So the next day, they went to the stables to give Aladdin and Midnight a chance to get to know each other.

When Aladdin came toward him with the saddle, Midnight jumped out of reach. When Aladdin swung up onto Midnight's back, the horse kicked up his heels. Aladdin went flying!

But when Jasmine climbed into the saddle, the horse did everything she asked.

It looked like Midnight was a one-princess horse.

Still, Jasmine's father wouldn't let her ride in the race.

The day of the race arrived. Riders from Zagrabah paraded into Agrabah, including Fayiz and his big gray stallion, Desert Warrior.

When it was time for the race, fans jostled for the best views. It seemed everyone but Jasmine was there to watch.

As they took their spot at the starting line, Fayiz and his horse looked confident.

Suddenly, Aladdin joined the line. He was riding a very strange-looking blue horse.

In fact, it wasn't a horse at all. It was the Genie in disguise!

The Sultan raised his flag. "One, two, three . . ." he called. "And they're off!"

The race was on!

A black horse with a mysterious veiled rider took the lead right away. As soon as they were out of view of the palace, the rider threw off the veil. It was Jasmine!

"I do hate going against Father's wishes," she whispered to Midnight, "but I had to prove that you were the fastest."

As the race went on, Jasmine stayed in the lead. But then Fayiz and Desert Warrior started to catch up! Jasmine urged her horse on, but Midnight couldn't seem to pull away. Warrior was big, strong, and *very* fast. Finally, he edged ahead of Midnight.

Jasmine and Midnight weren't going to let Fayiz win. Midnight galloped hard and passed Warrior.

"That trophy is Agrabah's!" Jasmine called over her shoulder with a laugh.

But Fayiz and Warrior weren't giving up either. They stayed right at Midnight's heels . . . until the horses had to jump a ditch that crossed their path.

Midnight sailed over it easily, but Warrior skidded to a stop, throwing Fayiz!

With Fayiz and Warrior out of the running, it seemed there was nothing to keep Jasmine and Midnight from winning.

But just then, Jasmine heard the sound of hoofbeats right behind her. They were coming up fast!

Jasmine turned back to see who was following her. She gasped. It was Aladdin! And there was something odd about his horse.

Soon Aladdin and his mystery horse had caught up, and he and Jasmine were fighting for the lead. Jasmine *really* wanted to prove that Midnight was the fastest horse in the two kingdoms and that she was the best rider. She pushed Midnight harder and harder.

As they neared the finish line, the two horses were neck and neck. First Midnight would pull ahead a tiny bit, then Aladdin's horse would take over. But neither could keep the lead.

The two horses crossed the finish line at the same time!

As soon as Midnight slowed to a stop, Jasmine jumped off. She gave her tired horse a hug and led him to the water trough for a drink.

Her father ran over. "Excellent work, you two!" he cried. Then he frowned. "Wait. Didn't I forbid you to ride?"

"I'm sorry, Father," Jasmine began. "It's just that—"

"Oh, never mind," the Sultan interrupted, grabbing the trophy and holding it up. "Agrabah is victorious at last! Twice over, in fact!"

Her father was right. Both she and Aladdin had won. She needed to congratulate him—and ask him a question.

She walked over to Aladdin, who was standing with his odd-looking horse.

"Congratulations!" he said when he saw her.

"Same to you," Jasmine replied. "But where in the world did you find yourself such a fast horse?"

Aladdin looked at his horse. Then he looked at his feet. He didn't seem to know what to say.

Just then, the Genie changed from a horse back into his usual form. Jasmine gasped. "Sorry, Princess," the Genie said with a wink. "We were just horsing around!"

When the Sultan realized what Aladdin had done, he frowned. The rules said only a horse-and-rider team could win the Golden Palm trophy. Aladdin and Genie were disqualified. And that meant . . . Jasmine and Midnight were the winners!

Jasmine patted Midnight proudly. Then she changed, and she and Midnight took their spots at the head of the victory parade. She had always known Midnight was fast. But she'd never imagined he was so fast that he could match the Genie for speed!

Fit for a Crown

Rapunzel was excited. After living in her tower for so long, she was finally free. With the help of her new friend, Flynn Rider, she had escaped from the evil Mother Gothel and discovered she was a princess. Along the way, she and Flynn had had many adventures.

Now they were traveling back to the kingdom. Soon she would meet her true parents, the King and Queen.

"I still can't believe *I'm* the lost princess," said Rapunzel as they walked along. "I don't even know how to be a princess."

Flynn smiled. "You have nothing to worry about," he said. "It's easy. All you have to do is wear a huge, heavy crown. . . ."

"Oh, my!" she exclaimed. Rapunzel grew pale. That didn't sound easy at all! What if it was too big? Or too heavy? She pictured the crown being placed on her head . . . and falling down around her waist!

Noticing how upset Rapunzel looked, Flynn tried to make her feel better.

"Do you remember that tiara from my satchel?" he asked. Rapunzel nodded. "Well, let me tell you a story about that."

Taking a deep breath, Flynn began. "When I was a boy in the orphanage, I read a book about a princess and her tiara. The book said this tiara symbolized everything the princess should be. The tiara's white crystals stood for a strong, adventurous spirit; green represented gentleness and kindness; red stood for courage; and the golden crown itself stood for leadership."

Flynn continued, "For years, I thought of that tiara, and then one day, I actually met a gal who could wear it. . . . "

As Flynn told his tale, Rapunzel's eyes grew wider and wider.

"The princess was certainly adventurous," Flynn went on, "and as she traveled toward her dream, she was kind and brave. She helped those who were hurt. And she was definitely a leader. She seemed to be able to turn every bad situation into something wonderful."

Rapunzel stopped Flynn. "Are you talking about—" she started.

"You!" Flynn exclaimed, nodding. "I'm talking about all those amazing things you did when you first left your tower in search of those floating lights."

"But I did all those things when I had long, magical hair," Rapunzel replied as they walked over a fallen log.

Suddenly, she slipped and almost fell. "Now I just feel off balance," Rapunzel added with a sigh. "I have no idea how to help anyone without my magic."

Before Flynn could reply, they heard a commotion behind them. "Nobody move!" somebody shouted.

Then several men came out of the shadows. They looked very dangerous. "Hand over your horse!" one of the men demanded.

Flynn leaped into action, chasing the thieves. "Rapunzel!" he shouted. "Run away, and don't look back!"

Rapunzel did not run away, though. Instead, she tried to rescue Maximus. She tackled one of the thieves and began to pull his hair.

Then she saw that Flynn had fallen in the water. Rapunzel ran over and pulled him to safety, and they continued to fight. Soon, the thieves were defeated.

When it was all over, Rapunzel turned to the leader. "You are *not* a nice man!" she scolded. "Stealing is wrong."

"I'm sorry, miss," the man said. He looked very upset. "I just needed your horse. You see, my son is hurt, and I don't have a horse to take him to the doctor."

"Oh my!" Rapunzel exclaimed. The man had been wrong to try to steal. But now she understood why he had wanted to take Maximus so badly. "Where is your son?" she asked.

The man quickly led Rapunzel, Flynn, and Maximus through the woods. They soon reached a clearing with a small cottage. Rapunzel rushed inside and saw a young boy lying on a bed. When she asked him what hurt, the boy held up his arm.

Rapunzel smiled. "You're a strong boy," she said. "I'm going to help you as best I can." Then she patted his arm gently—she knew just what was wrong.

She found a piece of cloth and made a sling out of it. Then she put the sling around the boy's arm. It wasn't perfect, but it would work until he could see the doctor.

Relieved, the boy's father lifted him onto Maximus's back. Flynn would give him a ride to the kingdom.

Watching Flynn and the boy, Rapunzel smiled. She had been worried that without her hair she wouldn't be able to help people. She realized she had been wrong. She had come to Maximus's rescue. She had helped the young boy. And she had even pulled Flynn out of the river.

Together, Rapunzel led Flynn, the boy, and his father toward the kingdom. When they arrived, Rapunzel finally met her parents. They held her tight, happy to have their daughter home at last.

Later, after Rapunzel had received her crown and greeted the kingdom, she asked her parents for a favor. She wanted to make sure her new friends would never have to steal ever again. Rapunzel wanted them to help the boy's family. The King and Queen agreed. They were so happy to have their daughter back. And even happier that she was such a kind, courageous, and adventurous young woman.

Belle and the Mysterious Monster

"Oh, dear!" Belle heard a voice cry.

Belle stopped in her tracks. She had been walking to the village square. As usual, her nose was buried in a book.

The voice belonged to Belle's neighbor, Madame DuBois. "There's a wild animal on the loose!" Madame DuBois exclaimed. "It ran through my yard and knocked down all my clean clothes. Just look at this mess."

"My goodness!" exclaimed Belle. "Did you see what it was?"

Madame DuBois shook her head. "No, but I heard it crashing through my garden. It sounded enormous."

After she helped Madame DuBois tidy up, Belle continued walking to the village. She kept a lookout for the creature, but she didn't see anything. Soon, she reached the bakery.

"Good morning Monsieur Le Pain," Belle said. "I'd like one apple pie, please."

The baker wrung his hands. "I'm afraid I can't help you today," he replied. "Haven't you heard? There is a beast on the loose! It ate all of the pies I left out to cool this morning. This one was inside, but it's for Madame DuBois."

Belle frowned. "That's terrible. I wonder what it could be?"

The baker shook his head. "I don't know. But a creature that hungry must be gigantic."

A little while later, Monsieur Marchand told Belle about something overturning his fruit cart.

"Did you see what it was?" Belle asked.

"It ran away too quickly," Monsieur Marchand answered. "But a creature big enough to knock over this heavy cart must be ferocious."

Belle thought for a moment. "If it's so large, it's strange no one has seen it." She bought some apples so she could bake a pie and went on her way.

As Belle started to head home, she saw Farmer Florent sitting on the edge of the town fountain. He looked very sad.

"What's wrong?" Belle asked.

"I am so worried," the old farmer said. "My little goat Babette is missing. I'm afraid that she might have been taken by the . . ."

"Wild beast?" Belle guessed.

"Yes!" he cried. "How did you know?"

"Because everyone in town is talking about it," Belle said. "But no one seems to have seen it. It's very odd."

Just then, Belle noticed a crowd had gathered in front of the village tavern. Curious, she walked over. In the center of the crowd was Gaston, the town bully. He was always bragging about his feats of daring and bravery.

“There is a terrible monster on the loose!” Gaston told the crowd. “Only a hero of great strength and smarts can stop it. Who among us is courageous enough to capture this creature?”

“Gaston, of course!” cheered Gaston’s friend, LeFou.

Belle spoke up. "But no one has actually seen it," she said. "Are you sure there is really a monst—"

"Oh, Belle, leave it to us, please." Gaston waved his hand.

But Belle had a hunch there was something more to the story. So she decided to do some investigating. First, she examined one of the ruined pies at the bakery. Then she found a half-eaten pear under the fruit cart.

Next, she checked Babette's pen. She walked around all the edges of the fence. Finally, she inspected the tracks in the mud by Madame DuBois's cottage.

After she had gathered all her clues, Belle was convinced she knew exactly what was going on. Now she just had to prove it.

Belle hurried home. She had an idea for the perfect way to catch the mysterious creature.

In the village center, Gaston and LeFou were also hard at work. The townspeople watched curiously as Gaston hammered and sawed an enormous contraption.

"Behold, my monstrous monster trap!" Gaston announced when he and LeFou had finished.

"It is guaranteed to capture the sneakiest, most dangerous monster easily," Gaston boasted. He swung his hand back to point to it.

"Wait, Gaston!" cried LeFou. "Don't—"

But it was too late. Gaston had accidentally hit the arm of the contraption, springing it!

Meanwhile, Belle had returned and set up her own simple trap. She placed a fresh-baked apple pie and a small pan of white paint at the edge of the town square.

Across the way, everyone went back to work while Gaston wiggled free from the net. He passed by Belle and laughed. "Oh, Belle. What good do you think a pie and some leftover paint will do to catch this wild beast?"

Just then, there was a loud rustling in the bushes nearby.

"The monster!" cried Gaston. He pulled a large club from his belt and jumped into the bushes. A moment later, he came back out, confused. "There was no large creature there," he said, puzzled.

Belle turned to look at her trap and gasped. The pie was gone! Something had snatched it while she was distracted.

And there was a trail of white footprints on the ground, just as she had planned. "Let's see where they lead!" Belle cried.

The townspeople began to follow Belle as she tracked the footprints. They went to a small cave at the edge of the forest.

Belle took a deep breath and went inside.

"Be careful, my dear!" called Madame DuBois.

"Yes, it could be ferocious," added Monsieur Marchand.

Soon Belle came out of the cave leading a small goat. It was still chewing some piecrust.

"Babette!" cried Farmer Florent. He rushed forward to hug his missing goat. "Were you the 'monster' all along?"

Belle smiled. "I had a hunch the creature wasn't big when I saw the little bites taken out of the fruit and pies," she explained. "The tracks in the mud were tiny, too. And there was a hole under the gate to Babette's pen. I thought it was Babette causing the trouble."

"How clever!" cried Monsieur Le Pain. "Let's hear it for Belle!"

"Hooray!" cheered the crowd.

"Lucky guess," Gaston muttered.

"Don't worry, Gaston." Belle smiled. "Next time, you can make your trap less monstrous, and it can catch the little monsters, too."

"That's not funny, Belle," said Gaston.

But the crowd laughed and laughed, because actually, it was very funny indeed.

The Great Cat-tastrophe

Cinderella stood in the dining room, carefully arranging fresh flowers.

"Beeea-autiful, Cinderelly!" her mouse friend, Jaq, said.

Cinderella smiled. "I just adore flowers." Then she sighed. "I wish I could go to the flower show tomorrow."

Once a year, the King hosted the Royal Flower Show for the village. Many unusual flowers would be on display. But Cinderella's stepmother, Lady Tremaine, never allowed her to go.

Just then, Lady Tremaine appeared in the doorway.

"Cinderella," Lady Tremaine said sternly. "What did I hear you say?"

"Well, I—" Cinderella began.

Lady Tremaine held up her hand. Then, an odd smile crossed her face. "So, you want to go to the Royal Flower Show? Well, I see no reason why you can't, as long as you finish all your chores today."

"Do you mean it, Stepmother?" Cinderella said excitedly. "Oh, thank you!"

Cinderella still had to scrub the floors, wash the clothes, and dust the furniture. But she was sure she could finish everything before the end of the day.

Just then, a fancy carriage pulled up in front of the house. Cinderella's stepsister, Drizella, shoved her other stepsister, Anastasia, aside so she could be out the door first.

"Girls, your manners!" Lady Tremaine cried. Then she turned to Cinderella. "Oh, I forgot to mention that the girls and I are taking Lady DuPont out for the day. Everything must be finished before we return at five o'clock. And dinner must be ready too."

Before Cinderella could answer, a footman walked up and handed Cinderella two fluffy cats.

Lady Tremaine smiled. "And you will also be watching Lady DuPont's cats, Precious and Treasure."

Cinderella brought the two cats to the sitting room. Lucifer, the family cat, followed her. Cinderella gently placed the pets on the sofa.

"How much trouble could two sweet little kitty cats be?" she said.

Then Cinderella went to work. She quickly dusted the furniture and scrubbed the floor. Next, she headed to the kitchen and popped a roast into the oven. While it cooked, she went outside to wash the clothes.

"All done!" she said as she hung the last piece to dry. "Now I'll just check on the cats."

“Precious? Treasure? Lucifer?” Cinderella called, opening the sitting room door. “Are you awake . . . oh, no!” she cried.

The sitting room was a disaster!

Feathers had been ripped from the pillows. The drapes were tangled. And dusty paw prints covered every inch of the floor Cinderella had just cleaned.

Cinderella sighed as she restuffed the pillows and straightened the drapes. Soon the room looked almost normal.

But the footprints were still everywhere. She would never be able to clean them all again in time.

"If only I had four hands for dusting . . ." Cinderella said. Suddenly, she had an idea. Quick as a wink, she grabbed a needle, some thread, and an old mop.

In a flash, Cinderella had sewn tiny mop shoes for the cats to wear! Once she had fitted them over their paws, she found a ball of yarn and tossed it onto the floor. The cats began chasing it around the room. Their shoes dusted the floor and furniture as they went without them even knowing it.

In no time, the paw prints were gone.

With the cats busy chasing the yarn, Cinderella went to check on dinner. Delicious smells filled the kitchen. The roast and vegetables were almost done. "Now all I have to do is keep an eye on the cats until everyone's home," she said, "and I'll be able to go to the flower show for sure!"

When Cinderella returned from the kitchen, she found the cats innocently napping on a windowsill in the warm afternoon sunlight.

"There you are," she said. The cats looked peaceful enough. But Lucifer was hiding something under his paw. Cinderella took a closer look. It was Jaq's hat!

"Lucifer, what have you done with Jaq?" she demanded.

The three cats snickered and glanced out the window. Cinderella gasped. The mice were huddled out on the roof.

"Oh, you mean things!" Cinderella scolded the cats. "You chased them out there, didn't you?"

Cinderella could see that the mice were too frightened to move. She needed to rescue her friends! After propping the window open, she carefully climbed onto the roof. She held on to a tree branch and made her way toward the mice.

This isn't so bad, she said to herself. It's almost like how I used to climb trees when I was a girl. I just won't look down.

"I'm coming!" she told the mice. "Don't be scared!" She reached out to them.

"Cinderelly to the rescue!" squeaked the mice.

They sighed in relief once Cinderella had placed them in her apron pocket. But just as Cinderella turned, she heard a loud noise behind her. *Snap!*

The cats had locked the window shut!

"What are we going to do now?" groaned Jaq.

Cinderella was stuck. There were no other windows she could reach. And the roof was too steep to climb down.

Bong! The castle clock began to chime. It was five o'clock. Lady Tremaine would be home any minute—and dinner was about to burn!

Just then, Cinderella noticed the clothesline she had used earlier attached to the windowsill. It stretched all the way to a tall tree in the yard. That gave her an idea.

"Everybody hold on tight!" she said to the mice. She took off her apron and looped it around the clothesline. "Next stop, the kitchen!"

By the time Lady Tremaine, Drizella, Anastasia, and Lady DuPont arrived, Cinderella was just placing dinner on the table.

"That looks delicious!" Lady DuPont declared. "And the house is sparkling. Lady Tremaine, was this the servant you were telling me about? I'd say she certainly earned the right to go to the flower show."

"Yes, I suppose so," Lady Tremaine said reluctantly.

"Thank you, dear, for watching Precious and Treasure," Lady DuPont said to Cinderella. "I know they can be a handful."

Cinderella smiled as Treasure ran past the dining room door, still wearing the little mop slippers. "Not at all," Cinderella said. "Actually, they lent me a hand."